Dedicated to my wonderful mother,
who always believed in me.

Shadows of Swartvlei

Leigh-Ann Ralph

A peopleMASSIVE book.
Published by Numba51 (Pty) Ltd

Copyright Numba51 (Pty) Ltd by Leigh-Ann Ralph 2023

Words by Leigh-Ann Ralph
Cover design by peopleMASSIVE

ISBN: 978-0-7961-2228-5

Numba51 (Pty) Ltd South Africa
34 Templeman Drive, Knysna Heights, Knysna,
Western Cape, 6571. South Africa
Reg. Number 2017/473496/07

PREAMBLE

Pain gripped her. She was confused, terrified. A fist slammed into her cheek, smashing the side of her lip against her teeth. Her mouth filled with blood. The blindfold hid the terror in her eyes, and the darkness disoriented her. Her captives laughed as they pulled at her clothes, pushing their clammy hands up her dress, groping her thighs.

"No! Leave me alone!" she screamed, her voice shaking uncontrollably as she fought desperately to get them off her. Someone punched her in the stomach, forcing her to buckle and collapse onto the cold, stone floor. An unforgiving blow forced the air out of her lungs. She fought for breath as her world grew darker.

I am going to suffocate, she thought. She tried pleading with them, gasping for words she couldn't speak as their raucous laughter drowned out her raspy sounds.

"I think I should show the bitch who is in charge," a deep, sinister voice said. She sensed he was standing over her, watching her squirm.

He was the larger of the two, with a scar running down across his right eye. His offensive sneer gave way to a substantial gap between his teeth which he continuously slid his tongue through as he sucked in air.

"Yeah!" agreed the other man.

The accomplice was average height with long, greasy, unkempt brown hair that trophy-shaped ears held back. His fingernails were chewed and dirty. The few teeth left in his mouth were decaying. His breath smelt vile as he tried to kiss her, pushing her hands above her head. She lay there frozen but relieved to be breathing again. Another vicious tug on her dress ripped the material and sent tiny Swarovski crystals flying across the room. She felt cold steel being pushed between her breasts under the base of her bra. With a flick of his wrist, the man with the deep voice used his knife to remove her bodice, exposing her breasts. She started to scream, but he quickly jerked his hand over her mouth, letting his body weight pin her down.

With his free hand, he grabbed at her breasts, and she felt him slobbering as he bit down on her nipple. Pain shot through her like a hot needle exploding in her brain. "Hey, it's my turn!" yelled his accomplice.

She let herself drift into the void where she knew she would be safe. She tried to push her thoughts away from her aching body. *Control your thoughts,* she repeated over and over to herself. Struggling under his weight, she felt his knee between her legs, forcing them apart.

Fuck, she thought, *this is really going to happen!* She began to pray. *You can't touch my soul. God will protect me.*

He fumbled clumsily, trying to undo his fly while keeping her still. She knew this and frantically tried to move away from his probing fingers. She bit down hard, sinking her teeth into his hand as he let out a loud shriek. His accomplice loosened his grip on her wrists and slapped her on the side of her head.

"Hold her still!" the man with the deep voice screamed.

"I'm trying to." he retorted, gripping her around the neck.

She started to gag as his thumbs pushed down on her windpipe, squeezing. The pressure on her carotid arteries was so intense she began to go limp under his arm. He quickly yanked her panties aside, driving his hip between her legs. She felt him climb up towards her groin. She wriggled hopelessly under his weight, screaming in her head. *This can't be happening. Please, God help me!*

A door flung open, and a shadow filled the doorway. An unfamiliar voice shouted over the chaos.

"What the fuck is going on here?" A man strode into the room and stared at the woman's red, swollen face. He didn't try to hide his rage at her presence and with the two morons he had picked for his purpose. *I should have realised that this woman would be more trouble than she was worth!*

He lunged towards the man with the scar, grabbing him by the hair and pulling his head back. The interruption caused him to release the woman for a moment. She couldn't see what she was doing, but with a fleet-footed kick, she caught him directly under his testicles. She heard the air forced out of his mouth, then a thump as he rolled over, clutching his crotch.

"Bastard!" she screamed, trying to cover her exposed body.

"Idiots! You'll ruin everything," the unfamiliar voice boomed again.

"We were just having a bit of fun."

"I told you to tie them both up. Now, take her back to the shed. We need them both alive."

He stopped, then added, "For now, at any rate."

The two men set about getting her to her feet. She started to say something, but her sentence was cut short as a sharp pain shot through her head. Everything went black. The man with the deep, sinister voice knocked her out cold with the butt of his revolver. They carried her to the shed, unlatched the door and threw her onto the straw.

"Oh my God! What have you done to her?!" a rough, dry voice filled the shed.

They ignored the man tied up in the corner, struggling against the tight, tied ropes around his wrists. They tied her hands behind her back. The man with the deep voice stood up, cursed under his breath, and kicked her with his foot, watching to see if the limp form lying face down in the straw would move. Nothing.

"Bitch," he snorted, kicking her again, this time on the thigh. He turned and walked out, leaving the tied-up man enraged while barely able to focus through a bloodied, swollen eye. He called to her, calling her name loudly, insistently... finally, gently. She did not respond. She lay very still – her face, pale. Blood trickled from her nose and mouth. Her bottom lip was bloodied and swollen. Her cheekbone was cut, with a purple and blue tinge marking a growing bruise.

He couldn't tell if she was breathing. He desperately needed to hold her in his arms and to tell her how sorry he was. His eyes fell on her naked breast. He hadn't noticed before. His heart started pounding; he squeezed his eyes shut. *Fuck! Did they rape her*? He felt desperate.

Vomit rose in his throat. His body began to shake. He stared at her beaten body. "How could I have let this happen!" he screamed angrily. There was a noise at the shed door. It opened, and the man with the deep voice walked in with a tray.

"You must eat! Boss's orders!" he said as he tossed the tray on a bale of hay.

"We can't eat with our hands tied," he spat.

"Yeah, right." He walked over and untied the woman first and then the man. "Don't do anything stupid now," he sneered and smiled as he turned slowly to face the woman, looking her up and down. "You don't want us to finish what we started with your girlfriend." He walked out laughing, latching the door once again.

Anxiously, he crawled over to her. He couldn't find a pulse. He quickly put his ear to her chest. *Thank God!* he thought, flooded with relief as he heard the rhythmical beat of her heart. He took off his jacket and covered her.

Carefully, he cleaned the blood off her face as best he could and gently lifted her head onto his lap. He studied every magnificent feature on her face and tried desperately to figure out how the hell he was going to get them out of this. Exhausted, he closed his eyes and fell into disturbed sleep.

He woke up with a jolt. She stirred. Her face grimaced as she sat up, holding the back of her head. She looked down at her torn clothes and shuddered.

"Are you okay?" he asked, concerned.

She spun round quickly, finding a familiar face in front of her eyes. She slapped him and began pounding his chest, screaming, "No damn it! No, I'm not okay!" She was scared but grateful he was there and terrified that he too was in danger. Gently, he pulled her into his arms and held her firmly while she sobbed.

"Everything is going to be all right," he reassured her while knowing they were both, in fact, in great danger.

Chapter 1

Lara lay still, eyes closed, pretending to be asleep. *Why did I drink so much of that 'fruity' blend last night? What shit*! she thought, resenting the fact that it was time to get up. *Urgh*, she thought. *My mouth tastes like vinaigrette left over from the bottom of the barrel.*

She let one eye pop open to scan her surroundings, assessing how much head-throbbing the light would cause. *So far, so good*, she thought, opening both eyes. She lifted her head, looking around very slowly. She pushed the duvet aside and sat on the edge of the bed, resting her head in her hands. Pushing her long blonde hair off her face, she stood up and ambled to the bathroom, yawning. She examined her face in the mirror. Her large, cat-shaped eyes were no longer misty grey and beautiful. Bloodshot eyes surrounded by puffy eyelids stared back at her. She suddenly felt worse than before. She hoped a morning cappuccino and a hot bath would sort out the dull headache and corresponding mood.

Lara Sheffield recently turned 28. She regarded herself as both self-assured and self-reliant. She seldom drank alcohol; however, when the mood dictated such, she would make up for lost time. She was ordinarily headstrong and always in control, but after one too many glasses of wine, she became loud and mischievous. Lara stretched, yawned, and turned the bath taps on. While running the bath water, she headed for the kitchen to turn on the coffee machine.

Lara lay in the bath, watching the steam float around her breasts. She stared at them peaking between the warm water and bubbles, thinking how jealous some women would be. Most women these days would pay good money for breasts like hers. But a reduction would be her preference! Lara stood five foot, seven inches tall; her body was firm and tanned. She boasted a flat stomach, shapely thighs, and a dynamite waistline. Her father had teased her as a child, forever telling her she was built for comfort, not speed. As she matured, her 'puppy' fat seemed to melt away, which changed her father's teasing into complete anxiety as the neighbourhood boys came calling.

The warmth of the water was comforting; she began to doze, remembering only pieces of what had happened the night before. The phone rang, breaking the silence. "Shit, it's late!" she cursed as she climbed clumsily out of the bath, ran to the room, grabbed hold of a towel on her way, and dove across the bed to reach her mobile phone on the bedside table. She read the name and considered whether she would answer. Of course, she would.

"Hello."

"Hey there, beautiful."

"Hi, Ryan. You certainly don't sound any the worse for wear!"

"Well, I wasn't the one who drank two bottles of Sauvignon Blanc chased by several creamy shooters," he pointed out, laughing.

"Oh, right, I forgot about those," she moaned. "Look, I'm not even dressed. I'm late, in fact. So, give me half an hour, and I'll call you back."

"Sure, chat soon."

"Cheers." She put the phone down.

Lara had spent the last couple of years getting her marketing and PR agency off the ground. She had pursued a career as a marketing executive in a corporate finance organisation in Johannesburg. While she loved the city and the people, something was lacking. The pace of the work always made her feel frantic. Some campaigns were good but not great. There were great ideas that never got off the ground. And she spent most of her time churning out newsletter after newsletter and hosting infinite business networking breakfasts. While the latter kept her busy, it was the big ideas and campaigns that she got out of bed for! She decided to give it up. Tired of the bureaucracy and the tedious red tape that came with it, never mind the internal politics in the race to the proverbial top, she decided to focus on a few key clients doing what she loved and walked away from corporate life.

She quickly earned her first few clients within a month of leaving her corporate job. Her reputation in branding excellence preceded her as did her innovative and fresh ideas. She planned to boldly market to an international client base as part of her twelve-month plan. Most of her clients were small, boutique businesses focused on health and lifestyle. Still, she was looking for that one big client, a client like JD Enterprises.

Lara rented a townhouse near to Rosebank. She converted it into a liveable office to save on rent. She wasn't struggling to make ends meet; she was intentional and careful with what she had. Lara's home was a good mix of modern furniture, with luxury (even if not expensive) carpets, throws and blinds in neutral tones.

Completing the look were touches of the continent she loved so much: bold colours of Africa, stone ornaments that celebrated fabulous weekends away, and black and white photographs from her safaris at Grietjie in the Greater Kruger Park. Her office space had the bare necessities: an Oak desk, leather chair, desktop PC, printer, and a bookshelf.

As Lara drove toward Rosebank, which was fast becoming the business hub second only to Sandton, she remembered she hadn't returned Ryan's call. Her mind was on her only appointment of the day. She arrived with time to spare. The building was impressive with huge brass lettering that read JD Enterprises. It gave the entrance an atmosphere of distinction. JD Enterprises was largely family-owned and managed by the Dillons – a family of success and wealth. If one let it, it could be intimidating. Lara had selected a cream-tailored suit and a light pink, silk strapped top while adorning her neck with pearls that added a touch of sophistication. Her make-up was soft and neutral, and her favourite perfume, subtle. Lara had her blonde hair loosely twisted into a loose knot. She certainly did not feel intimidated! Excited? Maybe. In control? Definitely.

"I'm here to see Mr Dillon," Lara said, smiling at the security guard.

"Certainly, may I have your name?" he prompted.

"Lara Sheffield."

"Ms Sheffield, please sign here," he handed her a register where she entered her personal and professional details. An ID card was scanned and given to her to clip on as a visitor's badge.

"Wear this identity card at all times," he said as he ushered through a turnstile.

"You'll have to take the elevator to the penthouse; you can't miss the reception area."

"Ta, thanks," she said.

Lara followed the security guard's instructions and stepped into the elevator of wall-to-wall mirrors. She pushed the button marked 'Penthouse,' checked her hair, and rubbed her lips together, ensuring her lipstick was even. A loud ping announced her arrival. She stepped out of the elevator onto white and grey marble floors. Two mammoth marble pillars stood proud on either side of the sliding doors leading into the offices. The reception area was a large crescent design with a central workstation and easy access to several other rooms or offices. The plush carpeting enhanced the heavy, slightly outdated mahogany furniture, while cream drapes softened the stark yet sophisticated decor. The artificial light gave the reception area a gloomy feel to it. The furniture was tastefully upholstered in bottle green, cream and gold striped fabric, adding a touch of earthy elegance. All the office automation fitted into cabinets that blended beautifully with the decor. Lara suddenly felt nervous.

A tall, thin, and rather daunting-looking woman stood at the photocopy machine to the left of the reception area. She looked up as Lara entered, peering over the top of her spectacles. She evaluated Lara as she walked over.

"May I help you?" she asked as if trying to stop her in her tracks. Lara took a deep breath, and with her head held high, she approached the reception desk.

"Hello, my name is Lara Sheffield. I'm here to see Mr Dillon." Lara smiled.

"Ah… yes, Ms Sheffield. I'm Mrs Perkins. Mr Dillon Junior is unfortunately detained and requested you meet with his father, Mr Dillon Senior."

"That would be fine, thank you."

"He can only spare 30 minutes of his time," she said, looking Lara up and down, then added, "I suggest you get to the point and not waste the little time you have with him."

Lara just smiled and nodded.

"Very well, this way, Ms Sheffield."

It is evident to Lara that this woman would not win a popularity award any time soon. Although she had to give the lady her due, she was direct and efficient, and she obviously ran the office accordingly. Lara straightened her skirt, checked her jacket buttons, took a deep breath, and followed Mrs Perkins into the office on the right. The woman stopped, turned, and pointed at a chair.

"Thank you," Lara said, almost gritting her teeth, feeling like a school child.

"Mr Dillon Senior will be with you shortly. Can I offer you some refreshments?" the eagle-faced woman asked.

Lara wanted to say, 'a jug of orange juice and two painkillers would be lovely.' Instead, she smiled, trying to forget her hangover. "Coffee would be lovely, thank you."

With a curt nod, Mrs Perkins swiftly disappeared, closing the door behind her.

The office atmosphere was in noticeable contrast to that of the reception. There was a mass of full-length windows overlooking the city. Sunlight filtered through and rested on the potted ferns selectively placed throughout the office. The décor was simplistic yet tasteful. The view took her breath away.

Lara did not notice the door opening. A rich voice filled the room, preceding a man's presence.

"Lara Sheffield? Joseph Dillon," he said, reaching his hand out to shake hers.

Lara had suspected there was an inter-leading door between private offices.

"Mr Dillon, lovely to meet you."

"Please, my dear, you make me feel my age. Do call me Joseph."

"Joseph, it is then."

"Come, please have a seat, Lara." He gestured her to a seat in front of his desk. "I expect Mrs Perkins will be in with coffee, so shall we get started?"

"Thank you," she said, remembering Mrs Perkins's advice. "I'm sure you will find my brand strategy diverse and fresh compared to the customary methodology."

"Well, let's hear your ideas," he said as he casually strolled to the window overlooking the bustling city.

"Joseph, what I'm about to share with you are the basics of any good brand strategy, so I would have to put a formal presentation together should we find common ground."

"Undoubtedly, Lara, so enlighten me." He wasn't about to make it easy for her.

Lara reached into her briefcase and pulled out her portfolio, aware he was toying with her. She cleared her throat and began, quickly finding her certitude. She took her time as she ran through her client work, success stories, creative ideas, and the overall strategy she envisioned JD Enterprises should take. Lara's confidence grew with each word she uttered. She could tell he enjoyed her creative ideas and her strategy's outlook!

Reading Joseph's body language, she noticed when her pitch piqued his interest and when it didn't. Even though he turned his back to her at one point, she knew he was a captured audience. She watched Joseph with keen interest while rattling off statistics proving return on investment and what she suggested they do.

Joseph turned from the window, pulled out his high-back leather chair, sat down, and listened intently to Lara. She reminded him of his late wife, May. The way she moved, her hands gracefully motivating each word as she spoke. He watched her facial expressions and gestures as she spoke and as she moved. She was intelligent and articulate and got right to the heart of their branding issue. She and her proposed solution were perfect for JDE's image change. She had spunk with a no-nonsense kind of attitude. And he had already done his due diligence. He knew a little more about Lara than she knew about him. She was one of the top people in her field. She lacked experience running a company of her own, but her reputation was stellar! She was just the person he needed, given what was coming.

The door flew open. Mrs Perkins glided in carrying a tray.

"Coffee, Sir," she announced as she placed the tray on the desk.

"Thank you," Mrs Perkins.

She didn't even look bothered that she had interrupted Lara's presentation. Mrs Perkins disappeared as quickly as she had entered. Joseph handed Lara a cup of coffee and gestured for her to continue. Lara felt surprisingly confident, and if she read this man correctly, her foot may just be in the door!

"In closing, Mr Dillon, I would like to say my current view is broad in that most companies of the size and reputation such as yours, are multifaceted." She was aware he was hanging on her every word. "It's important that the corporate brand does not change the facts but reflects them accurately and precisely." While closing her briefcase, she concluded, "I will start from scratch, keeping only the exceptional and throwing out the mediocre. Finally, we will work together to design and implement a corporate identity change and brand strategy for the JDE of the future."

"How long before you can have a proposal on my desk?"

"I can have a draft in two weeks; however, it will take several months to reconstruct your company's image and do the groundwork for the brand relaunch."

"Good!" he said, clapping his hands together and opening his diary.

"I'll see you in two weeks then; let's say Friday at the same time? I'll have the contract drawn up."

Lara flipped through her diary.

"That timing won't work for me. It will have to be the following week as I'll be in Knysna taking care of some business then." They settled on a day and time, taking a moment to relax in one another's company. They sat drinking their coffee, chatting about the Western Cape and the sheer beauty of the Garden Route. He mentioned that he had spent time there with his late wife. Lara didn't push him for more detail, and he didn't elaborate. He was a busy man. She put her cup down and smiled at Joseph. "It was lovely to meet you, Joseph."

"Likewise. See you in a couple of weeks then."

They both stood up. "I shall speak to my son and see if he can join us for the next meeting. He'll want to look through the contract and discuss it with you," he said, showing Lara out.

"Goodbye, Lara."

"Goodbye, Joseph and thank you for your time. I won't disappoint you," she smiled and left.

Lara was ecstatic! She had just landed that big corporate contract she needed for her business plan. The first thing she had to do was to speak to Ryan. She wished she could just pop in and give him the good news. Ryan Harding was unfortunately spoken for, the proverbial 'married man'. She had a heart-wrenching affair with Ryan for a few years. While she adored him, their relationship had turned from love to a mostly love-hate situation. She could talk to Ryan about anything and everything. He was indeed her best friend, but they both knew he would never divorce his wife, which was devastating for her. After years of anguish, love and tears, Lara realised there were depths of love and commitment. One she had, and the other belonged to his wife. Who was better off? That question remained one of the mysteries of the universe. Lara dialled his mobile phone and hoped that he was alone. She was relieved he answered, "Ryan, I got it! I got it!" she screeched.

"Hey, that's champion, congratulations," he responded with gusto.

"Let's celebrate! Dinner tonight, my treat?"

"Sorry, I can't. We must see the in-laws tonight."

Lara immediately became furious. He always managed to diminish her excitement.

"It's always 'we' Ryan. Remember, I'm not part of that 'we', except of course, when 'we' won't sleep with you, then I'm good enough," she spat, hating herself for being so foolish, so naïve!

"Why do you always…" he stopped. Another quarrel was in the making.

"What?"

"Nothing."

Lara hung up and hurled her mobile phone onto the couch. She grunted, clenching her teeth and flicking her hands in the air in anger. She tossed her head back and began to cry. Nothing about this relationship was genuine; she had spent so much time crying about Ryan. Walking away seemed an impossible task. Someone was unavoidably going to have to pay the ultimate price. Lara would never manipulate him into leaving his wife; that was his choice. Lara knew in her heart of hearts that it was time to hurt and give it all up. This had gone on long enough! She would do her best to ensure the heart-breaking journey was peaceful. She lay on her bed and felt miserable and elated simultaneously. It was time for new beginnings. She knew this was not the way to celebrate a new account. She leapt up and strode into the bathroom. Lara splashed icy water on her face and looked into the mirror. *Well, kiddo, it's just you and me… alone, once again.*

CHAPTER 2

Joshua Dillon sighed. Standing on the jetty, he sipped strong black coffee, gazing over the tranquil waters. Daybreak had always been his favourite time of the day. The water was calm, motionless. Its surface mirrored the sky perfectly, reflecting the light and making it look like liquid mercury. The air was cool. The only sound was the serenade of the weaver birds, busily building their nests. Josh had spent years at university studying Building Science to gain the kind of knowledge that was part of these little creatures' genetic blueprint. The construction of their nest fascinated Josh, as they were something of an architectural phenomenon. Finishing his coffee, he watched as the sun kissed the lake. The low, shapeless clouds would soon bring soft, fairy-like rain. Usually, Josh would be out in the middle of the lake with a fishing rod in hand, willing a Largemouth bass to take his lure. His grandfather had given Josh his prize collection of handmade lures that the old man had painstakingly designed and crafted. The collection had diminished over the years, and life never gave Josh the luxury of time to make his own lures. He found a local fisherman who made a reliable replica with the help of his grandfather's lure sketches. Josh felt it was the noble way to fish, rather than just buying the mass-produced lures at the local Knysna fishing tackle shop. As Josh watched the mist hover over the lake, he recalled his father, Joseph Dillon, telling him how the delicate olive and black-coloured fish were released into the small lake on their country estate, Chantilly. Chantilly, their family home, now Josh's home, nested peacefully on the banks of the Swartvlei Estuary, the largest and deepest lake in the Wilderness National Park. The Park was situated in the tiny coastal village of the same name, just a 30-minute drive from Knysna and in the opposite direction, the closest airport in George.

When Josh was a child, his father participated in buying a consignment of Largemouth bass, which were imported from Maryland in the USA. They were released into various local waters in the Western Cape in South Africa. He had released hundreds of small specimens into his own lake in 1937, and they thrived in the following years. Bass fishing was part of Josh's family legacy. A love for fishing was not the only feature he inherited from his father. Aside from a head for business, he had inherited the charming Dillon smile, wavy black hair, and the icy blue eyes. Josh and his father had identically shaped noses, which boasted a slight indentation on the tip, characteristic of the Dillon men. Their striking good looks constantly turned heads. Men were envious, and women were fixated. Josh had broad shoulders and stood six feet, three inches tall. He had a body that would put a twenty-five-year-old to shame. He worked out regularly and had the arms and abdominal muscles to prove it. Josh's ex-girlfriend described him as a self-centred, superficial, and domineering bastard. At thirty-seven, he certainly didn't have time for neurotic women. He was focused on helping his father run his multi-million Rand building company and taking time for some serious bass fishing. He didn't see it as selfish but as having his priorities right.

It began to rain a little harder. Josh turned towards the house, glanced at his watch, threw out the cold remains of his coffee and gave a short, sharp whistle. On the far edge of the Swartvlei, a sturdy red Staffordshire Terrier lifted her head. She bounded enthusiastically towards Josh, pausing only to bark at the Mallard Ducks that flew off into the lake's centre. She caught up with Josh at the house.

"Hey, little girl, are you through bulling the ducks?" he said, patting her head. As a puppy, she'd sit in a most un-lady-like fashion, boasting a watermelon-shaped tummy. Her skin seemed to wrinkle in small folds over her head, causing her to frown. Josh aptly named her 'Wrinkles'.

"Viens ma fille, let's see if Grace has breakfast ready for us?" he said gently.

Together, they walked up the stairs onto the patio and into the house. Josh loved living in Chantilly. Designed by his late grandfather, the main house was built out of solid logs. The rooms were spacious and well-lit. The yellowwood floors, window frames, doors and staircase came from the indigenous trees of the Knysna region. The decor was simple, with Karoo Mohair scatter rugs, sleeper wood furniture and an odd artefact collected by the Dillons over the years. Josh's mother had died when he was a teenager, and her portrait hung over the stone fireplace in the den. Her name was May Jean Chantilly. May was an alluring, voluptuous lady with cosmic blue eyes and long, blonde curly hair. Joseph always referred to her as his 'curvaceous Beauté'. He adored her. She was his life, his very lifeblood. The morning she died, Joseph said there would never be another May Jean. And there never was.

Josh finished breakfast, saw to his dog, and left instructions with Grace. He grabbed his briefcase and then jumped into his Jeep. He drove hastily through the woodlands, wondering if he had remembered to tell Grace to feed Wrinkles. Although she was not likely to be hungry after finishing most of his bacon. Josh reached for his mobile phone and dialled the pilot's number. "Steve! Josh here. I'll be on the landing strip in half an hour," he said with an apologetic note in his voice. He knew Steve, the company pilot, was a stickler for promptness. Josh knew he was late!

"Yes, Sir, we are fuelled and ready to go."

Josh smiled to himself as if there was any doubt. "Thanks, Steve."

As Josh headed to the airport, he thought about the three towns flanking Chantilly: Knysna, Wilderness and George. All three had a place in Josh's heart, each for their own uniqueness. Knysna was built around the tranquil lagoon waters. Twice daily, at the turning of the tides, the ocean water flowed in and out, filling and then draining the lagoon. It did so between two rocky, cavernous hills flanking the mouth of the lagoon, affectionately called *The Heads*. The crashing seas rounded off a spectacular view at the foot of The Heads. The name *Knysna* was derived from a Khoi word; locals had several theories as to the meaning. Josh's favourite was '*There is wood there';* boy was there ever. The Knysna forest was a little over 3000 square kilometres of tropical and subtropical moist broadleaf forests.

Sedgefield lay between Knysna and Wilderness. It was founded in 1894 when John Barrington purchased Ruigtevlei farm. He later named it Sedgefield in honour of his John Barrington – his father's – United Kingdom birthplace. Sedgefield had the best beaches, markets, and fishing, of course.

Wilderness, the last village before George (George, the closest town with an airport), was just like Sedgefield and Knysna. It too was home to vast, stunning beaches and majestic mountain hiking trails. The 'Map of Africa', a hilltop lookout point, was famous for its views of the Indian ocean, the Outeniqua mountains and the snaking Kaaimans river that formed what looked like the map of Africa from the highest point.

The nearby sprawling Garden Route National Park, a habitat for beautiful wildlife, including leopards, monkeys, and eagles, was loved by all who lived in the area. The fondly named 'Garden Route', a 300-kilometre green belt stretch of farm, wine, and forestland stretched between Witsand and the Tsitsikamma National Park and had so much to offer – all of which were right up Josh's alley. Josh pushed his foot down hard on the accelerator, leaning slightly forward in his seat, willing himself to make up lost time as he approached the George airport.

Josh entered the office and winked at Mrs Perkins as she handed him a cup of coffee. "Have they started?" he asked.

"Yes, Sir, about ten minutes ago. Your father is furious that you never made your meeting with Ms Sheffield," she whispered.

"Any messages?"

"On your desk, Sir."

Mrs Perkins handed him a copy of the agenda, "Shall I announce you, Sir?"

"No, no, I can manage my father. Thanks for the coffee."

Josh pushed the Boardroom doors open, "Gentlemen! Apologies for my late arrival."

There was a murmur of greetings. Josh caught his father's look of disapproval. Joseph called for order and declared the Board Meeting open. It was business as usual.

The Board comprised Joseph Dillon, the Chairman, majority shareholder and CEO, while Josh fulfilled the role of Managing Director. Saul Gerber headed the Architectural Department. Blake Henry was the Financial Director, and Peter Patterson was the Marketing Director. Joseph held seventy percent of the shares and the rest was equally divided between Josh, Saul, Blake, and Peter. Any legal matters were handled by Simon Fielding, cousin to Josh, who only attended meetings at the request of Joseph. Simon's family business law expertise came in handy given that JDE was a family business, the brainchild of Joseph. Joseph had awarded thirty percent of the shares to the managing force of JDE as a token for the long service given by each man present. Saul Gerber had started working for Joseph as a freelance architect right from the inception of JDE. They were inseparable. Together, they had built an empire and spent hours fishing at Chantilly. Saul Gerber was a stocky man, boasting a ginger beard that made him look like a Viking. His large brown eyes hid behind circular gold-framed spectacles. Saul was different from Peter Patterson, who was another kettle of fish. He was a tall, slim, unassuming gentleman with a receding hairline who always wore three-piece suits and paisley ties. He was a people person and forever a diplomat. His sandy blonde hair, hazel green eyes and hypnotic grin made him the perfect public relations professional. Josh employed him to manage HR marketing, advertising, client liaison and public relations. Peter was dependable and had everyone's respect – the salt of the earth.

Blake Henry controlled JDE's finances; although a highly qualified man in his field, he had little personality, austere looks and was a comprehensive introvert. A confirmed bachelor, he lived for work and had no time for people except his mother. Joseph had employed him as a favour to his late wife's sister. Blake was an only child dedicated to looking after his mother and JDE. Blake was a complex man to read but knew the exact financial situation of JDE by heart. He was an IT and computer wizard and had instituted several comprehensive securities and integral data-based programs for JDE management, linking to governmental municipal districts nationally. Blake had connected them via a network to always have local and international information at their fingertips. It was a joint venture that proved beneficial and lucrative to all parties concerned. JDE had completed significant building developments in partnership with the local municipalities, making Blake's work an asset. This was one of the reasons Joseph made him a partner.

"Before we continue our discussions for the day, I have something rather precarious to discuss with you all," Joseph said, looking around the table, studying each person for a sign of fear.

"For some time now, I have been trying to figure out why the opposition has gained an advantage over us regarding most building tenders. The figures specifically pointed to the last several months. We have lost two major contracts, which alone would have meant an extra R115 million profit this year."

"Dad? What's going on, what are you saying?"

"I'm saying we have a mole in our organisation!"

There were murmurs of disbelief from the Board Members.

"This is a big organisation. Dad?! You will have to be a bit more specific."

"What we have unravelled is at the highest management level, I'm afraid."

Saul was the first to react, "Joseph! I don't understand. You cannot possibly think that one of us is handing vital information to the opposition!" Josh threw his hands in the air, and Peter shifted uneasily in his chair.

"Gentlemen, please, before you all start shouting at once, hear me out; not only is this person selling our building development proposals, but has embezzled R123-million of JDE working capital."

There was a hush in the room. Each member looked at the other, wondering who could or would do such a thing. A bead of sweat broke out on Blake's forehead. He felt ill and confused. Peter's mouth dropped open.

"Blake! You're the Financial Director. How the hell is this possible?" snapped Josh.

"Are you accusing me, Josh?" Blake stammered.

"Of course not, but surely you picked this up, didn't you?"

Joseph broke in. "No! Blake never picked it up. It was an outside auditing firm, which I bought in to investigate the possibility of this happening. They did a forensic audit, and it's sad to say, I would have been none the wiser if I hadn't decided to do this. They worked at night under the semblance of a cleaning crew doing a deep clean of the building." Joseph looked at Josh's head, shaking from side to side and knew his son was about to blast him from a dizzy height.

"Why the hell didn't you tell me? I'm supposed to be the MD around here and, most of all, your son," Josh frowned and suddenly grasped why his father did not confide in him. "You suspected me?" he snapped, realising that his father had suspected them all.

"Josh, please, calm down. This is getting us nowhere. And no, Son, that is ludicrous," Joseph looked positively drained.

He was about to continue when the Boardroom doors opened. Mrs Perkins came in.

"Sorry to interrupt Mr Dillon, but the Police are here, what should…"

"The Police," Peter gasped.

Joseph cut Mrs Perkins short. "Send them in, Mrs Perkins."

Two plain-clothed Policemen walked in, gave a respectful nod to Joseph, and walked directly over to Blake Henry.

"Are you Blake Henry?"

"Yes, I am," he mumbled while he was pulled to his feet.

"You have the right to be informed of the charges on which you are being arrested. Most importantly, you have the right to remain silent, to be informed promptly of such right and the consequences of not remaining silent. Any information uttered or willingly given to an officer may be used against you in court..." his rights were read to him while they placed the handcuffs around his wrists.

Josh looked over at Peter sitting there with his mouth open in complete disbelief. It was the first time he'd seen Peter at a total loss for words in seven years.

"You can't do this to me!" cried Blake.

"You did this to yourself. It goes without saying, I'm revoking all company credit cards, taking back your shares, and you will lose all your benefits and profit share," hissed Joseph. I'm sure you will find jail titillating!"

"You can't do this to me! I'm family, and I only took what is rightfully mine. You planned to leave it all to your son after all my years of service. I've read your Will, and you left the entire company to Josh. What about me? I gave you fifteen years of my life!" pleaded Blake.

"You are going to live to regret this, Joseph."

Joseph kept his cool, glaring at Blake in disgust and couldn't resist adding, "Oh, by the way, Blake, you're fired."

"You're a dead man, Joseph!"

"Be careful, Blake. What you say now can and will be used against you."

The Police ushered a broken man out of the Boardroom. Blake turned and, in a hoarse whisper said, "You are going to pay for this!"

With that, they were gone.

"Close your mouth, Pete," Joseph said quietly.

Saul stood up. "I need a drink!" he said, walking over to the liquor cabinet. He selected a bottle of twenty-year-old whisky, poured a tot, and downed it in one mouthful. Joseph joined him at the back of the Boardroom and motioned to Josh and Peter to join him at the bar. No one seemed discouraged that it was mid-morning, and Josh made it official, "I think we can all use a drink."

"Okay – what I want to know is how he managed to conceal what he was doing?" enquired Peter, looking very distraught, "and someone tell me what the hell a forensic audit entails?" Joseph leaned against the Boardroom table and looked at the three confused men staring back at him. The look on Josh's face was one of fury.

"Okay, gentlemen, let's take a deep breath and I will tell you what I know," he said.

"This should be good," Josh's sarcasm did not go unnoticed.

"Blake deposited both Oaklands Mall and Cherrywood Complex's payments into the Trust accounts as he should. As the interest came through, he would immediately transfer it into a company expense account and carefully transfer smaller sums into an offshore account. A few days later, he would transfer that amount back. So, to an untrained eye, it looked in and out – done in error. He waited for the interest to be paid, then deposited the Cherrywood payment into the levies account. If somebody noticed it, he could plead ignorance or human error," explained Joseph.

"Couldn't amount to much, surely?" Peter asked.

"Because he did it numerous times, it mounted up quickly," Joseph said while sipping his whisky.

"No one would really question it, as we all trusted him with that job," Saul added.

"He was one of the family. We all believed in the prick!" Joseph said with disappointment in his voice.

"Blake got greedy and started doing it more often. I spoke to him about it, and he always had an answer. I did a little investigating of my own, and things were not stacking up. Then, a few months ago, I met this guy on the golf course who does forensic audits for a living. He suggested I go this route," Joseph revealed.

"It turned out he didn't make all the money fiddling bank accounts but by selling our tenders to our opposition," he divulged with sadness in his tired voice.

"Our percentage win rate had dropped, and we could not pinpoint why," Josh affirmed.

"The time and effort we put into each one of our tenders was a waste of time. All Blake needed was the bottom line," Peter remarked.

"Shrewd bastard," Saul said quietly.

"Yeah, only until you get caught. How could he believe he would get away with it? Our accounts are transparent, and it was only a matter of time. The annual auditors would have picked it up at the fiscal year-end," Joseph believed.

"Ah yes, but he chose his timing well. As the company accountant, he would ensure it would be several months to a year before sending it to our auditing firm," Joseph answered.

"Do you think he's threat is something we should be concerned about or not?" Peter said, directing the question at Joseph.

Joseph shrugged his shoulders, "He's looking at a long prison sentence. I don't think we need to worry."

"I can't believe you didn't tell me, Dad! Don't you trust me?" said Josh, frustrated. He poured himself another drink.

"Son, I could not tell you or anyone. The forensic auditing firm needed to hold all the reins on this investigation," he quickly added, "In fact, they insisted on it."

It took a lot of explaining on Joseph's part before Josh began to calm down. It was a shock for the entire management group, but Josh felt a great sense of disappointment. It would be Josh who would take over the company one day. *If a parent could trust you enough to take over a multi-billion Rand operation, why wouldn't he trust him with all this? What would I have done, given the circumstances?* Josh finally let his father off the hook, "Yeah, well, Dad, you did what was best for the company. Speaking of which, we have a position to fill. Any ideas?"

"That's my son, business as usual!" They all managed to laugh. The fact of the matter was that life would go on regardless.

Saul was shattered by the day's events. *Who would have guessed that old Blake could do something like this? They had lost a friend and a fine accountant. The look in his eyes as he left worried Saul. It was a look of absolute hatred. He had known Blake for too long not to be concerned. This was a man who never showed any emotion up to now. What did it mean?* He wondered.

Peter walked up to Saul and put his hand on his shoulder, "Saul... anything wrong?"

"Eh, what? No, nothing. Thanks."

"Well, gentlemen, Josh is right. We must look for a replacement for Blake. Josh, will you and Pete see to it?"

"Sure, Dad,"

"Peter, how are we going to manage the press?" Joseph asked.

"Well, Sir. I suggest we give a brief statement about Blake. At this stage, a 'no comment' might be construed as a cover-up; the press will have a field day with that." Joseph nodded in agreement.

"What about our major clients? We still have to close the amusement park deal with Sherman Corporation in Cape Town in a few weeks. Rumours could make or break this deal," cautioned Josh.

"What is happening with your overseas buyers? Are they still interested in building a hotel here, Josh?

"Saul and I have done all the spade work; our attorneys have drawn up the agreements, and we are good to go."

"That's the business side taken care of! Well done on brokering that deal. What about PR, Peter?"

"Perhaps we should have a pre-launch, cocktail party or social get-together? This way, we can deal with them all at once should questions arise," suggested Peter.

"I like that idea, but make it a formal event, and if Blake left us any money in the expense account, let's use it," Josh sniggered and continued, "I want no doubts that we are still in business and are here to stay."

"That's putting it mildly," Joseph said, raising his eyebrows, "I agree. Let's do it."

The rest of the morning was spent focusing on the general business at hand. Saul's architectural suggestion on how the amusement park would be suited to the environment and its people in the Cape took up most of the morning. Cape Town's modern, cosmopolitan city was surrounded by nature. Centered around Table Mountain, it was fast becoming one of the new Seven Wonders of the World. Cape Town, lovingly referred to as the Mother City, was widely revered for its beautiful beaches, stunning biodiversity, award-winning food and wine, and sheer variety of experiences on offer – all of which were incorporated in Saul's architectural design.

Josh reached out to his cousin and legal counsel, Simon, to discuss the predicament involving Blake. They decided to rendezvous at the Pig and Whistle, where Simon and his assistant Julian were already waiting. After deliberating, Simon concurred with Joseph's decision to take legal action against Blake for committing fraud and engaging in company espionage. In light of this, Josh felt more at ease and took the opportunity to acquaint himself with Julian. The drive home was peaceful as most peak traffic had petted off. It dawned on him that Simon and Blake were actually close friends. As much as Simon and he had spent time together as children, they were not tight anymore. *The childhood rivalry was a thing of the past, or was it?* Josh brushed the thought off, wondering if instinct made the thought cross his mind. Josh accelerated; he was eager to talk to his dad.

Blake was dazed. *This is crazy,* he thought. He stood watching each finger being pushed onto an inkpad and rolled firmly onto blocked white paper. Each print loops and arches in a different way. *How could they have found out? He'd been so careful.* Blake was exhausted.

They had given him the opportunity to phone his lawyer. On the advice of his lawyer, he had refused to answer any of their questions. After he was fingerprinted, he was placed in a holding cell. He lay on a hard mattress with his hands behind his head. Blake closed his eyes. *This is far from over, Joseph Dillon.* He fell into a restless sleep, dreaming of demons that enveloped him. The Board Members sat in judgment and bellowed the word guilty! Repeatedly. Joseph's laughter grew louder and louder as the demons placed a rope around his neck.

"Blake, Blake, wake up!" Simon called, shaking him by the shoulders. Blake's eyes opened; his ash-blonde curly hair was soaked with perspiration. He quickly sat up and wiped his face with the pillow.

"Must have had some dream," Simon remarked, handing Blake a cup of coffee.

Blake's hands were shaking so much he could hardly hold the coffee cup. He looked directly into Simon's eyes. He swallowed.

"You've got to get me out of here."

"Blake, I am not sure why you called me? I can't represent you!"

"Simon, I trust you and need your help!"

"Even if I wanted to help, I couldn't. JDE is my client."

Simon Fielding had been practising family business law for many years. He was not proficient in criminal law and told Blake to find suitable counsel. JDE was one of Simon's clients, which was a conflict of interest. And the case was to be tried in the High Court for which, Simon explained, Blake would need to hire an advocate specialising in criminal law. All he could do was put him in touch with two excellent advocates he knew personally. He explained further that for bail to be granted, his advocate would have to convince the High Court judge that he was not a flight risk. Blake's crime was serious. Blake would be remanded into custody if bail were refused until his trial date. Blake was not happy with Simon's counsel but realised it was futile. Unfortunately, Blake had left an incriminating trail a mile long. His only salvation was that this was his first offence, and up and until now, his track record was one of a solid citizen.

Blake had hidden the money in various bank accounts under fictitious names and in his mother's name, which couldn't be linked to him. That meant that Mrs Henry could post bail. *Now, all Simon had to do was stick to his word and find him an advocate so he could apply to the court to release Blake on bail,* Blake contemplated.

Although Josh lived at Chantilly, most of his time was spent in Joburg. JDE was situated in the business hub of Rosebank, and like all major centres, it was cold and impersonal, albeit impressive, with vast corporate buildings. As much as Josh hated staying in the city, he did enjoy the quality of time spent with his father. He was a fisherman and a hunter, but only when culling was necessary on Chantilly did he and his father enjoy hunting. His father taught him at an early age that you never kill anything that you weren't prepared to eat. Josh had become an expert at making game biltong and cooking freshly caught fish over an open fire. The Dillion men would never be seen in photos standing over their kills, rifle in hand. Culling was not about garishness.

The Dillon men were self-taught cooks; they shared kitchen duties on the days Josh was in Joburg. Joseph lived in a Spanish-styled home in a sprawling residential estate overlooking an eighteen-hole golf course. It boasted streams flowing into rock pools and delicate-looking cottage bridges, allowing access to the winding cobbled paths surrounding the fairways. Joseph's home's entire decor consisted of silk drapes in various shades of white and cream, with solid framed oil paintings of Cape landscapes painted by Dale Elliot adorning the walls. The cosy study with a stone fireplace was furnished with comfortable tub chairs and soft sofas. The kitchen was built in solid oak with white granite tops. Each of the three Victorian-styled bedrooms had ensuite bathrooms and a cosy sitting area. An open-plan dining room and lounge engulfed an Oak pub. The Rococo striped silk curtains and floral scatter cushions complemented the lounge suite, upholstered in designer diamond fabric. The oak dining room chairs were upholstered in bottle green and gold-stripped fabric, contrasting the soft off-white drapes. Although Joseph had a gardener and housekeeper, he still enjoyed pottering in his garden and impressing his friends with a few homecooked meals. He enjoyed entertaining, but, on most nights, he preferred the peace of the deserted golf course and Josh for company.

Josh arrived at the house just after seven that evening. He opened the front door to a familiar smell wafting through the house. *Onions frying in garlic butter! Dad is at it again,* he thought, putting the briefcase down on the entrance hall table. He loosened his tie while flipping through the mail.

"Great! You're home," said Joseph, peering out of the kitchen. "I'm making spaghetti bolognese!"

"Sounds good, I'm starved."

Josh walked into the kitchen and took a bottle of Cabernet Sauvignon off the wine rack. Joseph's eyes followed his son while he sautéed the onions and garlic.

"Not exactly the greatest of days, was it?" he said, trying to make conversation. He knew Josh was hurt because he hadn't confided him about Blake.

"You can say that again!" Josh said, pulling the cork out of the bottle with the wine opener.

Joseph added the minced meat to the sautéed mixture and began to laugh.

"What's funny?" Josh demanded.

"You're going to make me stew about this Blake mess, aren't you?"

"Dad! You could have trusted me; you undermined my authority and made me look like a complete imbecile in front of Saul and Peter."

"I'm sorry, Son, that was not my intention. How much more can I say? I said I'm sorry. What more can I do to make you realise I did the best I could at the time? Besides, my day was just as hard as I had to take your appointment this morning with Lara Sheffield," he reminded Josh.

"Couldn't have been that bad. You said we are going to hire her."

"I'm not sure I want her type of person taking over our corporate image".

"Why? What was wrong with her?"

"Not very bright, buck teeth, glasses, flat chest and big nose", Joseph said, laughing; his body quivered as if disgusted.

"Please!" Josh said, hearing the bullshit in his father's voice.

"Seriously, excellent proposal. Just wait 'til you meet her… Hell of a day." He added the chopped Italian tomatoes, parsley, and a dash of red wine and continued, "We have an appointment with her in two weeks."

"Sorry, I'm in Canada… Building Convention."

"Josh!"

"Well… I must go. I'm delivering the keynote presentation." It was Josh's turn to laugh, "I guess you're stuck with the ugly duckling."

Joseph smiled to himself. *It's my pleasure, you don't know what you're missing. He couldn't wait to see Josh's face when he finally met Lara.*

"Oh, if you insist!" Joseph said, sighing.

"You are full of shit, Dad. I know you wouldn't hire someone less than capable. So, she must have delivered an exceptional presentation at the very least."

Joseph quickly changed the subject, ignoring Josh's comment, "Can you believe the audacity of Blake – he actually asked Simon to represent him."

"No way. What did Simon say?"

"No, conflict of interest."

"Damn straight."

Joseph covered the mince sauce with a lid as it began to simmer. He followed Josh onto the patio. Josh had two crystal wine glasses in one hand and a bottle of wine in the other. The evening was warm. The moon hovered in the evening sky, gently touching the shimmering swimming pool water. Josh handed a glass of wine to his father. They sat staring at the moon for a minute. Joseph turned, looking at Josh, "You will be back for the cocktail party?"

"Yeah, wouldn't miss it."

"Why don't you fly back with me this weekend, Dad?"

"Ah, I could do with a weekend at Chantilly."

"Well, come with me. We fly to George on Friday."

"Next time. I'm playing golf with Saul this weekend."

"You play golf every weekend, Dad".

"When last did you catch a fish? Besides, I think Grace has the hots for you."

Joseph giggled, "Hmm, that she does."

"You are avoiding her, aren't you?" The phone rang.

"Saved but the bell." Joseph leapt up and went to answer the phone.

Josh laughed and knew when to let it go. He heard his dad chatting away in the distance. He lay back on the bench and closed his eyes, trying to make sense of what was an exhausting day.

CHAPTER 3

Lara picked at her food. *What is the point?* She thought. She loathed eating alone. She wondered what Ryan was doing. *Playing house again, what a farce!* She felt weepy. *Pull yourself together, Lara.* She pushed her food aside; sipping her coffee, she started reading the JDE information booklet that Joseph had given her earlier at their meeting. As she read, she began to make notes for her brief. The more she read, the more excited she became. Ideas began to emerge, titillating her creative side. The phone rang. It made her jump.

"Hello," she said.

"Hi, Sis," Stacey said cheerfully.

"Stace! Hi. How are you?"

"Fine thanks… Are you packed?"

"Ready to leave!"

"What time is your flight on Friday?" Lara reached into her bag and pulled out a copy of her ticket.

"Arriving in George at 15h30."

"I'll be waiting. Prepare to party, girl."

"Hey, I'm on a working trip, remember! I've got a client to see, and I'm working on a brief for a new client with a weekend in between." Lara explained, laughing.

"Yes, Sis! But, like you, I wouldn't miss out on an early morning horse ride, so I got to run. See you Friday!"

"Bye, Stace."

Lara was from a small family. Her parents owned and ran a boutique shop situated in Knysna Central. They had spent their entire married life in the quaint little town. Stacey and Lara were born eighteen months apart; they were shipped off to Boarding School at an early age. This made them inseparable until Stacey married the town's most eligible bachelor and settled close to Knysna. Lara went off to college in Johannesburg. But they spent every opportunity they could together. Having a client in the Garden Route who was prepared to fly Lara in every three months was a bonus. Lara was sure Stacey had something to do with her getting the contract. Lara's client was, of course, Stacey's husband, Robert Rowan.

Robert had the idea of running courses dealing with all aspects of sailing. Teaching the youngsters the basics: theory, wind awareness, rigging, sailing on all points of sail, positioning yourself in the boat, steering, tacks, gybes, docking, mooring, anchoring, launching, and trailering. Robert secured a bank loan, and together with a small inheritance, he purchased a small fleet of fully equipped yachts. Robert had the necessary qualifications but never had a clue on how to market the idea. Lara had given him a little advice. Robert was so impressed he hired her on a three-year contract to put his idea to the public.

Lara suggested calling the company 'The Sea-Seals', which became an overnight success. Lara was busy negotiating with the tourism Board to sell the attraction to the international market. She would have the answers she needed by the week's end. So, it was, by all accounts, a significant business trip.

Lara's thoughts turned to Ryan Harding. Tossing her notes to one side, she strolled over to the liquor cabinet and took out a bottle of her favourite white wine. *Great! Now I'm drinking on my own. Why hasn't Ryan phoned me? I'm sure he is deliberately trying to drive me crazy,* Lara thought, pouring a glass of wine. *Time to do something about you, Ryan!*   Lara dialled his office number.

"Hello."

"Hey stranger, why haven't you phoned your favourite girl?" Lara teased gently.

"Sorry, you must have the wrong number," Ryan whispered on the receiving end. The line went dead. Lara's mouth dropped open.

"Bastard!" she screamed, slamming the phone down. Lara knew Ryan's wife had to be with him, and as usual, Lara had to take the brunt of it. *I've got to be out of my mind to put up with this shit.* It was humiliating, to say the least.

The question on her mind was naturally, *why did she continue to contact him?* Lara took a gulp of her icy wine, making her quiver. She began to cry again.

She closed her eyes, forced back the tears and prayed for peace in her life: *Please, dear Lord, don't let this destroy me. Surely, 'knights in shining armour' do exist outside of the cinema. All I want is a little love and affection and not to be used.* Lara sipped her wine. *Then again, why should you listen to a woman who is having an affair with a married man and drowning her sorrows in a bottle of wine?*

She suddenly felt very alone.

Ryan knew he was tormenting Lara and was aware she would be fuming about now. He wished he had the nerve to leave his wife; Ryan did not love her in the way he adored Lara. She was a good wife and mother to his children. Divorcing the mother of his children would alienate him from friends and family. Financially, she would crush him. *I'm too old to start over again. I wish Lara would understand that as a fundamental choice between his wife and Lara. Lara would win, hands down. Sadly, it was not that simple.* He desperately wanted to phone her back to apologise for being abrupt, but he knew it would be wise to wait. She needed to cool off. She always did. He also knew that with his wife snooping around, it would have to wait.

"Ryan!"

"What?"

"I asked you a question?" said his wife with a frown on her face. "You are miles away,"

"Sorry, what did you say?"

"Are you ready to eat? I made your favourite."

"I'll be there in a second... thanks," he said quietly, wondering what Lara was doing. *How could I possibly give my family up? Even if it means lying a little to them both, I could never change the situation without someone getting hurt.* Ryan knew it was a selfish attitude to take, but until he was forced to choose, he would continue regardless.

CHAPTER 4

Peter grinned. He enjoyed his job. A social gathering was sure to lighten the pressure, given the shocking week they were having. JDE's employees were appalled at what Blake had done; rumours infiltrated the corporate sector like bad publicity had a knack for doing. Naturally, most of the gossip couldn't be further from the truth. Peter remembered when he and Mrs Perkins had been absent the same day, and by the end of it, the rumour was that they had a secret rendezvous. For a second, he imagined that. A*ah! Not in this lifetime.* He looked up as Mrs Perkins walked in with documents to file in his cabinet. He burst out laughing.

"Sorry, Sir, did you say something?" queried Mrs Perkins, peering at Peter over her gold-rimmed spectacles, as she was so fond of doing. Peter's eyes widened as if he had been caught stealing from the cookie jar.

"Er, private joke. Was thinking of an associate of mine, you know," he mumbled, trying his best to cover up. Mrs Perkins cut him short with a curt, "I understand, Sir."

The phone rang, alleviating Peter's awkwardness, "Patterson, hello."

"Pete, Joseph here."

"Yes, Sir, what can I do for you?"

"How is the get-together coming along? Are we organised?"

"I'm busy with confirming arrangements now. We are set to go," assured Peter.

"Pete, do me a favour. Add Lara Sheffield and a plus one to the guest list. I'm sure Josh mentioned she was doing some consultancy work for us," Joseph cleared his throat and continued, "This would be an ideal opportunity to introduce her to Josh and the rest of the staff. Josh confirmed he would be back from Canada."

"Yes, he will be…I checked his dates with Mrs Perkins."

Josh had told Peter about his dad's meeting with Ms Sheffield, and apparently, his father had said she was an ugly duckling. From his tone, that was putting it politely. Pete was tempted to remark about her unfortunate looks but decided Joseph would not be amused, so they said it would not be a problem.

"Listen Pete, I want you to go the whole hog on this. Spare no expense; we could all do with a relaxing evening."

"My sentiments exactly, Sir. Leave it to me."

Peter cherished the idea of entertaining clients and creating events that spread a little happiness. In his own life, he lacked the ability to achieve this for himself. His imposing good looks did not bring tranquillity to his world. He was what one would call a 'lady's man', but if a woman got close, he would run in the other direction. Committing to a relationship was not a priority in life. It terrified him. It was easier to stay away from any well-intentioned woman than it was to give her the benefit of the doubt.

Josh would mock him by saying that the 'mushy stuff' would get him in the end; it would only take the right woman. Peter wished he was more like Josh. Women just flocked to him like bees to pollen. The only difference between them was that Josh took it all in his stride. He seldom got involved. On the other hand, Peter jumped in with both feet and then left with his pants in hand, running for the door! He was not heartless, so he carried that guilt.

Saul walked into Peter's office, hands in his pockets, which was a dead giveaway. He had something on his mind, "You got a minute?"

"Sure, what's up?"

"I wanted to ask you what you thought about this whole Blake saga."

"What's there to think about – the man is a crook, and he will pay."

"Did you hear what he said when they dragged him off?"

"Empty threats, he was trying to have the last say, that was all."

"I'm not convinced of that. The day they arrested him, he had a look in his eyes I've never seen before."

"Actually, it gave me the chills, come to think about it," Peter said hoarsely and quickly added, "He is still in jail, you know."

Saul took his hand out of his pocket and rubbed his neck, "Not for long. I believe his bail hearing is this week."

Peter reclined in his chair, turning a pen in his fingers, "What does Joseph think?"

"He thinks I'm worrying for nothing. Do you think we should be concerned with his threats?"

"I worked closely with Blake for a few years. He's a puppy. He made a mistake. And he is paying for it. From what I hear, he is going to spend a great deal of time behind bars," Peter reassured Saul.

With that, Mrs Perkins walked into the office. "Excuse me, Sir, but here is Ms Sheffield's contact number. Mr

Dillon said you will need it," turning to address Saul, she added, "Mr Gerber, please don't forget your ten o'clock appointment with Mr Dillon Junior."

"Josh! I nearly forgot," Saul said, springing to attention, "See you later, Pete, and thanks."

"No problem, anytime."

Pondering over what Saul had said, Peter decided to do some investigating of his own. He picked up the receiver and dialled.

"Hello, gorgeous?"

"I do not believe this, a blast from the past. So, Pete, to what do I owe this pleasure?"

"I need some information, and perhaps we could discuss it over dinner tonight?"

There was a giggle on the other end of the line, "Info I can get you, but it's been two years. Pete and I gave up on you a long time ago. I'm a married woman now."

"Ah no, really? Lucky guy. Congratulations!" he cheered and cautiously continued, "Well then, I'll get to the point. I need some information and was hoping you could help?"

"What do you need?" she said in a girlish tone.

"Can you find out what is going on with Blake Henry, who was arrested for fraud earlier this week?"

"Sure, do you have an ID number for me?"

"Yes, I'll text it to you."

"That's great, I'll be in touch."

"Thanks, Mrs Gorgeous," said Peter. He heard her shriek with laughter, and the line went dead. He stared out the window for a minute, remembering how shocked he was at Blake's defiant look as the Police marched him out of the Boardroom. *How could anyone possibly blame Saul for being on edge?*

Josh and Saul spent the entire morning going over designs and discussing current projects. The largest of all was the Sherman Project in Cape Town, which was due to be finalised.

"Are the final drawings done for Sherman?" Josh said, looking at Saul, who looked preoccupied, "Saul!"

"Sorry, Josh. What was the question?"

"Are we set for our meeting with Sherman when I get back from Canada? Any hitches I should know about?" repeated Josh.

"We are ready, but he has changed his mind again about the landscaping."

Josh took a deep breath, "What now?"

"Sherman wants the entire building, car park and entrance surrounded by white rose bushes. This would involve demolishing the natural Fynbos."

"I can't believe he wants to destroy the natural vegetation for an English country garden. Do fucking roses even grow in that area?!"

"I've looked into it, and I agree, the approach is not logical."

"Do me a favour, phone this damn pilgrim and suggest that because of the high rainfall, he should consider a combination of Fynbos, indigenous ferns, and selectively placed palm trees. There are about five indigenous palms to South Africa; he can take his pick."

Saul laughed and nodded in agreement.

"Thanks, Saul."

"Lunch is on me this Friday," Saul said, packing up his documents.

"Let's reschedule. Steve is flying me back to George. I'm spending the weekend at Chantilly and leaving for Canada on Sunday."

"You sure do get around Josh. You must love aeroplane food or something," he laughed as he said goodbye.

CHAPTER 5

At last, Lara closed her eyes. Smiled. *This is the life.* The aircraft thumped onto the runway; tyres screeched as they touched down on the tar. The engines hissed as the compressed air was forced out. The plane's speed instantly decreased. Clicking sounds ran simultaneously through the cabin as people unfastened their seat belts. As the aircraft reached the terminal building, Lara stood up, gathered her belongings and made her way to the exit.

She wondered what her sister would have in store for the weekend. She could only guess that apart from a horse ride, it would involve a pub, Knysna's famous oysters and plenty of local Mitchell's draught.

Lara spotted Stacey standing on the far side of the baggage area, waving frantically. Lara grinned and waved back. She grabbed her suitcase off the turnstile and pushed through the crowded airport.

Stacey was shorter than Lara, with shoulder-length hair that shone like a copper pot hanging over a fireplace. Although the sisters were different in many ways, their eyes had the same enchanting effect – significant, blue, and breathtaking.

"Tart!" screamed Stacey, "Aah, it's so great to have you home."

They hugged each other; Lara gently pushed her sister away and said, "You look beautiful, Stace."

"What can I say? I'm stunning… it runs in the family," she appreciatively gestured by throwing her head back laughing.

"How's my favourite brother-in-law?

"Well, as husbands go, he's the best… but…" Stacey hesitated, looked around and whispered into Lara's ear, "As a business partner, he sucks."

Lara chuckled, "Well, that is what I am here for. I'm not going to let my favourite client, who happens to be my brother-in-law, project a company image that sucks!" Lara linked arms with her sister and quickly added, "Now, take me to your leader."

The beauty of Knysna captivated all who passed through the town, and Lara was no exception. She always felt a sense of peace each time she returned to Knysna. Unfortunately, the same could not be said when leaving. Lara thought that a big part of her being stayed behind, maybe even the best of her. It left her with a sadness she could never quite understand. The evening that followed went well; Stacey had arranged a family gathering with their parents. They naturally chose the local Seafood Tavern, Tapas on the Jetty, which was on a jetty overlooking the Knysna lagoon. The lagoon was formed 180 million years ago when the earth's continents were separated by around 300 meters of water. The Knysna Heads, the headlands of two peninsulas, enclosed and formed the Knysna River Estuary, affectionally known as the Knysna Lagoon. The Estuary measured about three kilometres, and at The Heads, which is the Knysna River mouth, it measured just 230 meters wide. The incoming tide flowed through The Heads at a rate of between 1,000 and 2,000 cubic meters of water per second and reached 17 kilometres inland.

Stacey and Rob lived on a small holding on the outskirts of Knysna, on which Stacey fulfilled her childhood fantasy of having a ranch where she could stable horses, have wide open spaces for her kids to grow up on and grow her own vegetables. Stacey always boasted that dreams do come true. Hers did. Rob loved the farm, but sailing was his life and his business. The Sea-Seals kept him extremely busy. The farm was a handful, so Rob had a reciprocal relationship with Vossie, his neighbour and his sheep. In return for letting his sheep graze, Vossie took care of maintaining the boundaries and doing the odd jobs his business would not allow Rob time for.

At dawn, Lara got out of bed, put on a pair of denim jeans, tucked in her white cotton shirt, and pulled on an old pair of Stacey's leather riding boots. She had just completed platting her hair when Stacey pushed the door open and popped her head in, "Ready to go?" she whispered.

"You bet. I've been looking forward to this all week."

They arrived at the stables to find the two horses saddled and ready to go. Stacey was the more accomplished horse rider of the two sisters, so she rode Rob's black stallion, Nugget, and Lara rode Stacey's horse, Porridge. She was the colour of oats with a beautiful temperament, which suited Lara, who was not a great horsewoman.

The horses trotted steadily down towards the south boundary gate and crossed the dirt road into an open field of natural fynbos. At this time of the year, the meadows were covered in a carpet of tiny sprigs of purple and yellow blossoms, joined in harmony with lush green foliage.

"I'll race you to the edge of the woodland," challenged Stacey.

"Ten bucks says I'll whip your butt," answered Lara with a smirk on her face.

Before either woman could respond, the horses leapt forward into a gallop. Lara felt the wind in her face. Porridge's robust and muscular body shifted with ease as she bolted through the long grass; her gold mane bounced to the rhythm of each stride she took. Lara watched Nugget dart in front. She could hear Stacey egging Nugget on, so she leaned forward, holding her head level with Porridge's, hoping to incite her to catch Nugget. Stacey aimed for a colossal log lying across a small stream, knowing that this would slow her sister down somewhat. Nugget leapt into the air, clearing the obstacle with little effort. By the time Lara realised what was happening, she felt Porridge spring forward in an up-surge motion as she jumped over the old log, spraying water from the stream around them like a fine mist. Lara lost her stirrup, and she almost lost her balance. Gripping Porridge firmly with her knees, managed to hold on, clutching the horse's mane. Lara's heart pounded painfully in her chest as she tried to find her stirrup. The last time she had attempted a jump like that was when she was in her teens. Lara looked up and watched Stacey slow down and circled around to face Lara. She had won by almost three full-lengths. Porridge broke off her stride, snorting breathlessly.

By the time Stacey came to a halt, she was chuckling, "Pay up, Tart!"

"Yeah, right, later, when I get my breath back," Lara said, holding her chest. "I damn well nearly fell off, and you're laughing!"

"Nobody told you to follow me. Besides, it was a tiny log. You're just a baby."

"This 'baby' will beat you one day," Lara looked around and pointed. "What's beyond that fence?"

"Private property, I would imagine."

The horses shifted restlessly.

"Let's take a look; there are no signs."

"Lara, I said, it's private property!"

"Now, who is the baby?!"

"Shit, you are relentless," teased Stacey as the horses trotted towards the boundary. Once she reached it, she bent over, lifted the gate latch, and nudging Porridge forward, they pushed the gate open.

Lara turned to look at Stacey, who was shaking her head, "Close it after you." Stacey did not say a word, but Lara knew the look. Stacey watched Lara and Porridge disappear into the dense forest, knowing Lara was going to try and hide from her.

Piece of cake, she thought.

Lara waited for the forest to close behind her, pulled the right rein, and pushed her heels into Porridge's side. Porridge broke into a steady trot and followed the path that went off to the right. *Let's see if you can find me,* she thought, smiling to herself. She gazed up at the enormous trees. The warm sun filtered through the leaves. The forest was steaming, and a leaf would periodically fall, floating gently down the path in front of Lara. She could not help but be amazed at the size and variety of ferns that grew in the forest.

Porridge slowed down into a walk and tried every now and then to munch on passing forest plants. The horse's hooves crushed the leaves on the forest floor. Lara wrinkled her nose up, trying to identify the different smells permeating through the forest. She was thinking how damp and mystical the Knysna forest could be and wondered if all the legends were true about the forest people and the Elephants when suddenly the forest opened, and Lara was faced with an enormous body of water.

Startled at first, the sudden warmth of the sun urged her to pull the reins in to bring Porridge to a halt. Lara knew it was far too big to be a dam and too wide to be a river, so it had to be a lake of sorts. Stacey was sure to know. She looked around to see if her sister was following. Lara tried to get her bearing as the forests can confuse the issue. The largest body of water was probably Swartvlei, but she was sure that they were nowhere near there.

So, where did this lake come from? Lara was puzzled and intrigued.

Lara dismounted, tied Porridge to a nearby tree and walked over to a rock close to the edge of the water. Her eyes scanned the horizon; she could see a small clearing on the opposite side. At first glimpse, Lara almost missed the log home that was camouflaged by the forest.

She was busy contemplating going for a swim in the freshwater when her eye caught sight of a fishing boat hidden in the reeds. Curious, she carefully moved closer to get a better look. A man was sitting in the little boat, fiddling with his fishing rod. He looked up and in Lara's general direction. She instinctively ducked behind the rock and held her hand over her mouth... *Shit! Had he seen me?* she thought apprehensively.

Ever so slowly, she peered over the rock, but he was looking away. Lara watched him stand up in the boat, which she guessed was about six feet tall. He was so close to her that she could see him put his fingers in front of the reel and hold the line with his index finger. He reeled the line in so that the lure was at the tip of the fishing rod. He angled his body towards his targeted area and swiftly gave a power stroke, simultaneously releasing his finger. The lure struck the water, rippling the surface ever so slightly. Lara was fascinated with this man and his focus. He retrieved his line and repeated the action. This time, she saw him strike, reel in, and a black and silver fish wriggled at the end of the line. Lara wanted to cheer for the fisherman but held her breath instead. The man was not alone as the dog gave an excited bark. A little Staffie was trying its best to get hold of the fish. The man scooped the fish into a net and landed it in the boat. Lara stared at this man as he continued with his seemingly agreeable task.

"What are you doing?" a hoarse whisper exploded in Lara's ear. Lara jumped, surprised. It was Stacey crouching next to her. Lara had forgotten all about her.

"Shit, you gave me a scare!" she said, pushing her sister over. Quickly putting her finger over her mouth to hush her to be silent, Lara pointed in the direction of the boat.

"Hmm...nice," Stacey said, peering over the rock.

"Do you think he's married?" Lara murmured quietly.

"Knowing your luck, he has several wives. How should I know? Besides, it never worried you before."

"That's a shitty thing to say. Ryan and I never planned to fall in love; it just happened."

"True, these things happen. If you are in love with him, why are you playing peeping Tom on private property?"

"Keep your voice down. I think he's cute, and a man that names his boat G&T is a win in my books," Lara said, giggling like a schoolgirl.

"I think this is really perverted," Stacey said in protest, "Let's get the hell out of here before we get arrested!"

"Spoilsport!"

"Really?" Stacey muted, tapping her watch. Lara realised that they were very late for their breakfast meeting with Rob.

She nodded, "Okay, I'll meet you at the gate," Lara took another quick peep over the rock and followed Stacey. *What are the chances that I will see him again? Shit, he is cute! Eat your heart out, Ryan. This may just be a sign!*

Fishing gave Josh time to think. Mainly, he concentrated on catching the ultimate-sized fish. But today, his mind was on his trip to Canada, on the one hand, and the problem with finding a replacement for Blake on the other. JDE had three possible in-house promotions that Josh still had to discuss with his father. That would have to wait until he got back from Canada. Josh planned to leave for Canada on that Sunday evening. He would be away for only a few days. Josh hated all the travelling he had to do and decided to make it a mission in his life to hand over some of the overseas trips to Peter. *That's what managerial appointees are supposed to do: make one's life easier.* Josh knew that it was easier said than done.

Over the years, Josh had been to Hong Kong for the World Congress on Urban Growth and the Environment, the International Exhibition for Environmental Technology and Services in France, and now the International Environmental Landscaping Conference in Canada. Only this time, Josh was to be a guest speaker at this closed convention in Winnipeg. JDE was one of the Top 20 Global Building Project Companies and believed in environmental landscaping as a priority in the building industry. The Convention was aimed at innovative technology, ideas, and concerns.

Josh had spent almost an hour casting and retrieving before he had caught anything. When he did catch a Largemouth Bass, it was a fair size, and Wrinkles' barking was all the applause he needed. Josh was about to cast out when he suddenly looked up. *I'm sure there is someone on the shore. I must be getting jumpy in my old age,* he thought as he cast out. As he reeled in, he said, "Gotcha," under his breath. This was number two for the day and as always, Wrinkles barked with excitement.

Josh couldn't shake the feeling that he was being watched and decided to call it a day.

"Well little girl, once we get these two beauties cleaned, Grace can cook them for lunch." Wrinkles wagged her tail as if she knew exactly what he said. Josh pulled in the anchor.

As they approached the house, they saw Grace standing on the veranda with her hands on her hips. "Don't you for one minute think you are going to scale those in my kitchen basin again."

"Of course not, wouldn't think of it." Said Josh. *Certainly not after the last time that is,* Josh thought as he smiled and changed direction.

"Joshua, your father phoned."

Josh stopped in his tracks. "Yes?"

"Trouble with that Blake chap. He said you must phone him."

"Did he say what kind of trouble, Grace?"

"He skipped the country or something. Jumped bail is what he said."

"You're kidding!" the expression on Grace's face changed, and he knew she wasn't. *I don't believe the nerve of this man. He is full of surprises.* Josh made a mental note to beef up security. *Knowing Blake, he's long gone by now. Had we known him at all, we would have seen this bloody mess coming.*

"Come on, little girl, we've got fish to clean," *and bigger fish to fry.*

Grace was like a mother to Josh. She was a voluptuous woman with auburn hair, green eyes, and porcelain doll-like skin. Josh imagined she must have been a beauty in her heyday. She was initially employed as the caretaker of Chantilly when his mother passed away, but over the years, she became part of the family. She certainly treated him like a child, but he had a lot of respect for her. With Grace in his life, he knew he would always have a comfortable home and great food on the table.

"Okay, little girl, let's get this fish to Grace. Then we can go for a drive to Brenton and take a run on the beach," Josh had decided he needed the exercise, and a swim in the sea wouldn't hurt either.

"Grace, would it be in order if we had a late lunch today? I have a hankering to go swimming."

"Better before you eat, young man, than after. Lunch will be at 15h00, no later."

"Thanks, Grace. You are a star."

Lara's meeting with Stacey and Rob had gone well; they made a lot of progress in deciding what kind of international marketing would be workable and who the actual target markets would be. They had worked right through lunch, and Lara was pleased with the results, but most importantly, Rob was very enthused by all her ideas. They called it a day.

Lara desperately wanted to feel her feet in the sand and thought a walk on the beach would do her the world of good. Without too much fuss, she left the rest of the family and headed for Brenton. Lara parked her car and stood for a moment, looking over the cliff onto the white, sandy beach. The wind had picked up slightly, and she could feel it blowing through her hair. *I hope it's not going to be too windy on the beach.*

Steadily, she climbed down the steep timber stairs to the beach. The thought of climbing back made Lara frown. The descent was bad enough.

Lara was suddenly grateful she kept herself in shape. She stepped on the beach, wriggling her toes in the sand, chuckling as she felt the sand's course yet comforting texture. A shiver ran down her spine. She began to walk to the water's edge, strolling in the direction of Buffalo Bay.

Before Lara realised it, a wave crashed on the shore, and white water rushed towards her. She misjudged its strength, and water surged up her legs. Lara let out a squeal and tried to avoid being soaked. The water had shot between her legs, just managing to wet the crotch of her white denim shorts. The cool water left a trail of sand and salt, leaving her feeling silly and somewhat messy. Retreating to a safer distance, she took a deep breath. Lara relished the smell of the ocean – especially today as the beach was quieter than usual, except for a handful of hotel guests ambling peacefully in the sun, an odd little crab scuttling for shelter, and a jogger seemed to fade into the distance.

Lara found a comfortable spot near the rocks. She dug in the sand, made a mound for her head to rest against, and carefully placed her towel. *No one is near my spot,* she thought as she looked around. *I'm secluded; who would even notice that I'm in my underwear and not a bathing suit?*

Lara unbuttoned her shorts, hung them over the rock and made herself self-comfortable. The sun was warm on her face, and there was a slight breeze. Lara folded her tank top up so that her stomach would tan. She felt comfortable that from a distance, no one would be any the wiser as to her lace panties, but from close, it would be another story – they were particularly revealing. Lara searched the beach for people. All was clear. She settled into a comfortable position and made a dangerous mistake. She closed her eyes.

After jogging for a few kilometres, Josh welcomed the cool sea water crashing around him, diving into each wave engulfing his tanned body. Josh swam out just beyond the breakers and turned to see what Wrinkles was up to. She was bounding down the beach, in and out of the water as it rushed ashore. Josh continued swimming along the shoreline, stopping only to catch sight of Wrinkles.

Wrinkles scurried, sniffing whatever was in her path. Every now and then, she would change direction and bound towards an unsuspecting Seagull. Josh slowed down and turned to make his way back to the beach. He caught sight of Wrinkles changing direction and ran towards someone lying near a rocky outcrop on the soft white sand. Josh knew that Wrinkles would never hurt anyone; at worst, she would make a nuisance of herself. Wrinkles had taken one look at Lara and raced in the direction of the napping woman.

Lara woke with a fright, confused at first with this sturdy little dog on top of her, licking her face. Without thinking, she jumped up and tried her best to ward off the enthusiastic dog. Realising her attacker was trying to lick her to death, she started to laugh. It was then she heard a voice behind her.

"Wrinkles! Down!" Josh shouted.

Lara spun around and stared at the half-naked man, water dripping from his broad shoulders down his tight torso. The sight of this man towering over her made Lara a bit giddy. Her mouth dropped open as she caught her breath. Everything seemed intensified. Lara sensed that time had come to a standstill. She saw the man's mouth moving, but she could not hear anything. All her focus was on the wet curls that danced around his forehead and his tanned, muscular chest that expanded with each breath he took. Lara focused on a dimple in his cheek as he smiled at her. She slowly looked up into his icy blue eyes. Mesmerised, she stepped back, nearly losing her footing.

"Sorry about this," he apologised, grabbing the dog's collar. "She tends to get over-excited in open spaces, especially on the beach."

"Huh, um, no, it's not a problem," fumbled Lara. Her mouth felt dry, and she was battling to compose herself as she smiled awkwardly.

Josh smiled back. Lara watched his eyes drop, and at that instant, she blushed, remembering her lace underwear. Lara had little time to decide on whether to grab her shorts or towel; she turned and bent down for the towel. Lara knew in a flash that it was the wrong move. *Shit, I am wearing a G-string, and this man is obviously focused on my butt,* she thought as she wrapped the towel around her waist. When she looked at him again, he was standing with his arms folded, rubbing his chin with a grin from ear to ear. They both started laughing with uneasiness. *Lara wanted to curl up and die from the embarrassment of it all.*

Josh spoke first. "I must apologise. Wrinkles loves people, and she…"

"Don't be silly. No harm is done; she is a delightful little dog," Lara said as she launched into an explanation as to why she was standing there in her underwear.

Josh smiled. "I have no objection to you wearing your G-string on the beach," he said, watching Lara turn scarlet. He quickly added, "Still, I would like to make up for the intrusion. Let me buy you a cup of coffee. It is the least 'we' can do."

Lara watched him pat his dog, "Wrinkles insists. Coffee and a jam scone?"

"Sounds perfect!"

They strolled back to the Brenton Hotel, stopping off at Josh's Jeep to collect dry clothes and a lead for Wrinkles. They sat outside on the hotel's deck overlooking the now deserted beach. They ordered two cups of coffee and a bowl of water. They spoke in general about the weather, the magnificent view and, surprisingly enough, not about each other.

CHAPTER 6

Blake drove slowly down a winding dirt road. He was shaking. He was nervous. Yet, he felt exhilarated. For the first time in his life, he felt alive. The thought of merciless revenge was a definite turn-on. Blake shifted in his seat; the ache in his groin made him uncomfortable. Blake knew that his life had taken a hundred-and-eighty-degree turn and that there was no turning back. *It's ironic,* Blake thought, pleased with himself, *young Winston Churchill had used the same Witbank area as a haven during the Anglo-Boer war, having escaped from a Pretoria prison, and here I am, a lifetime after, a fugitive.* His face beamed with delight.

Blake took profound enjoyment in the fact that he had outsmarted the Police, his lawyer and even his dear, old mother. He felt a twinge of guilt because he would miss her. She was the only woman in this world that made sense and who loved him unconditionally. His father was never more than a passing thought. Blake never cared much for him. Right now, Blake's mind was intent on destroying everything Joseph Dillon cherished, and he would ensure that Joseph would suffer the pain of loss and humiliation.

A few years back, Blake had bought a weekend retreat from an associate who had bought it under a Closed Corporation. His associate had died two years ago, and Blake knew that the cabin could never be traced back to him. He never even told his mother about the cabin, nor did he have neighbours that he had ever met over the years. It was perfect! The new hideaway was roughly a hundred kilometres east of Pretoria along the Oliphants River and well hidden from the water's edge.

Blake had carefully planned his escape, what it would take to change his identity and to fool the Police into believing that he had left the country. Blake was an IT prodigy, and his ability to find what he needed using his hacking smarts meant it was going to be as simple as a push of a button.

He pulled up outside the rustic wooden cabin, quickly unpacked what he needed from the Panel Van and parked it in the shed attached to the cabin. It was too late in the day to re-spray the van, and Blake was eager to change his identity.

Blake busied himself with setting up his computer and getting the sparsely furnished cabin into a liveable habitat. One thing Blake was not short of was cash. He had made sure that 80% of the money he took from JDE was well hidden in bank accounts or in gold Kruger Rands. The cash transfers were in place, and it was a matter of time before it landed in his new bank account in the name of 'Winston Van Niekerk'.

Two men and a woman holding a camera stood on the patio and pushed the button to ring the doorbell. It took a few minutes before an elderly lady appeared at the door.

"Yes?"

"This is Detective Sergeant Ed Matsinye and Officer Jansen from the South African Police Service (SAPS), and my name is Mike Phillips. I'm an attorney investigating your son's case. We need to ask you a few questions concerning the whereabouts of your son," he explained as Ed flashed his badge.

"I do not know where my son is. I am sorry. I can't help you at all," Blake's mother said without making a move to open the security gate she was standing behind.

The two men glanced at one other, and Ed firmly said, "Mrs Henry, your son is a fugitive. He has committed a grave crime, and you could be charged with aiding and abetting if you are unwilling to cooperate with our investigation." His voice changed as he watched the old lady's face pale, "Trust me, we do understand your loyalty to your son, and we are not here to upset you. We just need to ask you a few questions."

"Very well, come in," Mrs Henry said, leading them into the sitting room. "Can I get you something to drink?"

"Coffee would be great, thank you, Mrs Henry," accepted Mike, while Ed merely nodded respectfully. Officer Jansen kept her distance.

The tiny silver-haired lady disappeared into the kitchen, leaving Mike and Ed standing awkwardly in the lounge. Picking on little old ladies was not the best part of Police work, and it always left them feeling like neighbourhood bullies. Mike picked up a framed photo of Blake and had to wonder why an intelligent man like Blake Henry would resort to fraud.

"That was taken when he graduated," Mrs Henry's voice filled the room. Mike almost dropped the picture; he wasn't expecting her back so soon.

"Please help yourselves to milk and sugar".

Ed spoke first. "When last did you see your son, Mrs Henry?"

"Yesterday, his lawyer friend, Simon Fielding, said that he was going to pay Blake's bail and that he would be home that afternoon. He only came home late that evening. He ate the supper I had kept for him, and he went to bed."

"What did you discuss with him before he went to bed?"

"I asked him why he had taken money from Joseph, and he had said that it was money owed to him and I believe my son. He would never steal from anyone."

"Did he give you any reason to believe he was going to leave?"

"No, he was tired and acting a little peculiar, but I thought he was only trying to get my finances in order. He said if he was convicted, he wanted everything to be in order. He was worried that I wouldn't have enough money to look after myself. You know, he always took such good care of me after his father left."

Mike cut her short. "Did he make any phone calls before he went to bed?"

Mrs Henry started to look a bit bewildered at all the questions. "I'm not sure. He has a mobile phone, you know."

"When did you discover he was gone?" Ed said, standing up.

"This morning, I found a note."

Mike quickly interrupted, "May we see the note."

"Yes, here it is," she said, taking it out of her pocket.

Ed made a gesture towards the note and said, "May I?" Mrs Henry nodded.

Mike began to read the note aloud. '*My Dearest Mother. I am truly sorry for hurting you in any way, but I must leave the country. Arrangements are in place with Simon Fielding to take care of you. I will always love you, Mom! Your devoted son, Blake.*'

Ed Matsinye looked up to see tears running down Mrs Henry's face. *He hated this job! Why did women always have to cry?*" Mrs Henry, we'd like to look in Blake's room if we may?"

They followed her up the stairs onto the landing of an open-plan studio. There was an adjoining shower, hand basin and toilet. It was furnished simply with a double bed, dresser, and a desk. Ed was making notes. He said, "Mrs Blake, is there anything missing from the room?"

Officer Jansen's camera was clicking loudly at a fast shutter speed. Time was limited. She wasn't about to miss a shot.

"I'm not sure. I haven't had a chance to look," she said, frowning at the flashing light. She looked tired and annoyed.

Mike could see she was lying, but he knew that they had overstayed their welcome. Ed was about to insist that she check, but Mike cut him short.

"Thank you for your cooperation, Mrs Henry. We may have to come back at a later stage. Perhaps you can make a list for us."

As they got into the car, Ed said that the last phone call made from the house was to SA Airways, and if he was in a hurry to leave the country, why would he take his PC? A laptop, perhaps, but not a desktop.

"Okay, I give up. How do you know he had a PC in his room?"

Ed grinned. "Dust!"

"Dust?" Mike frowned as he reversed the car out of the driveway.

"There was a mark on his desk. He definitely had a desktop, which he took with him when he left."

Mike shook his head, "It doesn't make sense... It makes you wonder what he needs an old desktop hard drive for when he's got millions to play with," he pushed his fingers through his hair. "I can't help feeling this is all part of a bigger scheme."

Blake had not grown a beard in years and couldn't believe that it was growing out so grey. Shaving his head was the hard part. He pierced both his ears with a needle and pushed in gold sleeper earrings. He inspected his new looks in the mirror and felt it still wasn't enough; he remembered the bottle of gold theatre paint he bought. He painted one of his top teeth gold. He pulled a face. *You look like pirate Winston Van Niekerk. All I must do now is gain ten kilograms or so, and nobody will recognise me.*

Changing the shape of his body and his looks was the problematic part for Blake; he had prided himself on keeping trim and healthy. The fun part would be changing identity documents, hospital records, and his passport. All he needed was his old PC and a good printer. This was a hobby of his when he was a student. While the other students spent their evenings chasing women, practising the art of seduction, he practised the art of forgery. It was no big deal in those days, just student cards and the odd driver's licence, which he did for fun for those few people who bothered talking to him. So, all he needed now was the programme in his hard drive that he had created years before. As soon as he got all the information and essential data he needed, he planned to dump the computer at the airport. This would really confuse the Police, as Blake knew it was a matter of time before they searched his house and discovered his PC was missing. *They would certainly question his motives for taking it out of the country.* Blake turned the computer on and typed in his password. The screen came alive, and he selected the file named 'Tommy.doc'.

Chapter 7

Lara's head was throbbing. The Champagne had really taken its toll. Coffee and jam scones turned into a bottle of Champagne and fresh oysters. This gorgeous man who she had just met was incredible. He was intelligent and gentle. The thought of him gave her butterflies in her stomach. After coffee and goodbyes, Lara drove her car steadily towards Knysna, oblivious to the traffic behind her. *I can't believe that a man like this would even give me the time of day, let alone take me out again.* She tried reasoning with herself as best she could. *If someone had said, 'Lara, what kind of man would you like to spend the rest of your life with?' I would have to say, 'This Man!'* She suddenly realised she didn't know his name. *That is crazy... How on earth do you have a few drinks with a stranger, watch the sun go down and not introduce yourselves?* Lara's heart sank. *What if he forgot her phone number or wasn't serious about phoning?* Lara shook her head; she was not about to let anything spoil her mood. This was a knight in shining armour. He was strong and a gentleman! *That would mean he had to have a few faults. There you go again, trying desperately to find something wrong with a seriously gorgeous guy. You stay in a relationship with Ryan for what? It's going nowhere. He only brings you heartache. No, not this time. You are through punishing yourself.*

Lara's mood instantly switched over, and she felt inspired. This time, she was determined that if this man contacted her, she was going to go out of her way to encapsulate him in the profile of her so-called life.

Lara arrived at Stacey's house only to find a note saying they had to leave for an Angling Club meeting and would be home late. Lara was relieved. She made herself a cup of coffee, had a hot bath and went to bed. She lay staring at the ceiling, wondering what Ryan was going to say when she told him she was getting married and moving to Knysna. A giggle caught in her throat. The thought of watching him throwing all his toys pleased her. She was wondering how her knight in shining armour would react to her plans and if he knew about Ryan.

Lara switched the light off and snuggled dreamily in a foetal position. She felt totally relaxed and almost didn't hear the phone ring.

"Rowan residence, hello," said Lara, holding her long hair back.

"So, it's Ms Rowan, is it?"

Lara gasped; her heart began to race, "No, not quite. It's my sister's surname," she said, fumbling again over what was supposed to be a long overdue introduction. "Do you have a name?"

"Some people call me JD, and as he said Josh, the line went dead for a second.'

"Jade?" Lara said, struggling to hear what he had said.

"Close enough," Josh answered, laughing.

"So, Tanga! What do they call you when you're not running around on the beach in your underwear?"

Lara blushed, incredibly grateful that he couldn't see her face, "Lara... Lara Sheffield."

Josh almost dropped the phone. *Surely this wasn't the Lara 'ugly duckling' Sheffield his father had moaned about; the Lara Sheffield that was now in charge of the company's corporate image.*

"Lara! Wonderful to make your acquaintance." She really took him by surprise. *Lara Sheffield!* He tried as best he could to mask his shock and quickly said, "How would you like to meet me at Tapas for a drink?" Josh fumbled over what was a well-rehearsed invite to lunch and promptly added, "...say twelve thirty tomorrow?"

"I would love to have a drink with you, Jade."

"Good. I look forward to getting to know you, Lara Sheffield. Sweet dreams, Tanga."

The line went dead, leaving Lara with a sense of warmth running through her very essence. Josh smiled as he hung up the receiver and softly said, "Gotcha, Dad!" He was going to correct Lara when she called him Jade instead of JD. He wasn't quite sure why he didn't tell her what his real name was, but something stopped him. *Just as well he didn't, as it would spoil things if she knew he was her new employer.* He didn't want to run the risk of her dating him for the wrong reasons or dumping him either. It was never easy for women he dated to come to terms with JDE and what went with being a Dillon. He didn't like misrepresenting himself, but he really liked this lady. For once, he wanted to find out if a woman would find him attractive even if he were a struggling artist or a travelling salesman. He would have to think of something in a hurry. This was one lady he wasn't about to let slip through his fingers. His thoughts turned to his dad and the harmless lie he had told concerning the 'Sheffield Swan'. His mind began to plan his revenge. Josh grinned at the thought of Lara looking suitably embarrassed when she realised her snow-white butt was showing. It had been a long time since he had seen a woman blush. *She is stunning,* he thought. *Just play it cool, Josh, don't stuff it up.* He knew in his heart that lying was not a smart move. *You may live to regret that move, Jade! Jade who?* Josh thought about it and decided on Smith. 'Jade Smith'. Josh looked up at the portrait of his mother and said, "You would like her mom; she's got spunk." Josh grinned. He had it all worked out.

Lara woke up early, considering it was a warm Sunday morning, and it was the only day she could have to enjoy a little lie-in. Somehow, she had that feeling that one gets as a child on Christmas Eve. Something good was about to happen. She stretched out her arms and said, "No, something great is going to happen."

"You look bright and chipper this morning," Stacey noted as she walked in carrying a steaming cup of freshly percolated coffee. Her eyebrow rose slightly when she saw the smile on her sister's face. "I give up, what?"

"Stace, he phoned me."

"Who phoned you?"

"Jade."

"Who the hell is Jade?" Stacey said in frustration.

Lara jumped up and danced around the room, "I met him yesterday on the beach. We are having a drink at Tapas today. He is wonderful. I want to have his children."

"Oh shit, I've heard enough," Stacey grabbed a pillow and covered her face, she was laughing hysterically. "You have a plane to catch tonight, so if you are planning to have his babies, may I suggest you start right away," she laughed so hard that tears ran down her cheeks. She watched Lara's expression change as she put her hands on her hips, "What is so funny?"

"Nothing, I'm sorry, sorry-" Lara watched her sister push her face into the pillow as she tried to stop herself laughing. Lara's eyes softened, and she began to see the funny side. She grabbed another pillow and hit Stacey over the head. The war was on. Pretty soon, they were having a full-on pillow fight. One of the pillows burst, and feathers blanketed the room. The storm of feathers filtered through the air, resting on everything in the room, including the sisters. They both screeched with horror as they watched tiny white feathers float gently around the room. The door burst open, and Robert flew in, "Are you okay? What the…" he stopped, and the concern on his face turned to an *'I'm not amused at all'* kind of look. "I would suggest you both clean up the mess while I make breakfast."

"Don't be a fuddy-duddy, darling. Lara is in love."

"Good for her, d-a-r-ling. Could we eat before the wedding!"

Lara threw the pillow at her brother-in-law as he left the room.

"You not invited!" Lara teased.

"Alright, he's gone, tell me everything."

Tapas was built on the Thesen Island jetty, overlooking the Knysna Lagoon. Tapas was a rustic restaurant with a stunning location. Looking at the wooden, nautical-themed décor and vintage photographs and maritime memorabilia, one couldn't help but be transported to earlier times when Thesen Island was a timber processing hub. Known initially as Paarden Island, it was named after the horses that grazed on its pastures. In the early 19th Century, the island became a hub for timber processing. Purchased in 1870 by the Thesen family – a Norwegian family of timber merchants – they established a sawmill and shipbuilding business, which flourished for many years. The island's importance grew, and it became a bustling industrial centre with its own power station, school, and even a movie theatre.

This famous Tapas restaurant had a perfect view of The Heads in the distance. If one sat at a window seat, it was like sitting at a bar counter in the middle of an open sliding doorway to the salty lagoon waters.

Josh arrived a little early and chose a seat with the best view. The glare from the water was comforting, and this way, he could catch a tan before leaving for Canada later that evening.

Lara sauntered into Tapas feeling self-conscious, which was out of character for her, but 'Jade' made her a little on edge, to say the least. She lingered for a moment to scan the room for him. He was sitting at a window in the sun; he looked up and waved. She was grateful to see that he, too, had opted to dress casually. Josh wore a baggy pair of blue shorts, which matched the colour of his eyes, and a white loosely fitted T-shirt. By the time she had reached him, he had put on a pair of sunglasses. Lara suddenly felt naked without her sunglasses and made a mental note to put them on as soon as she sat down. *It was apparent no one was going to give any secrets away easily.*

"Hi Jade, have you been waiting long?"

"Hi there, little lady… just got here. What can I get you to drink?"

"A little white wine will be great, thanks," Lara shifted on her bar stool, trying to get comfortable and ever so casually placed her sunglasses on.

Josh returned with an expensive bottle of Sauvignon Blanc and poured a glass of wine for her. "I thought we could get something to eat while we are here."

"That sounds great... hmm, this wine is delicious."

"It's actually from one of our Estates..." Josh quickly cut himself short.

"Our Estates? Are you in the wine business?" Lara said with interest.

Josh looked at her and thought for a second that perhaps he should tell her the truth about JDE. "Heavens, no... I meant it's a South African wine. I'm an artist, actually."

"Sounds very romantic. What do you paint?"

"A little of this and that, your regular boring stuff."

"What medium and style do you use?"

"Medium style?" Josh knew then that he had picked the wrong thing to lie about.

"Well, I-"

"Come on, all artists are shy about their work, but you had to be influenced by one of the great masters, or are you into the new age pop art?" Lara said, laughing.

"Claude Monet had what it takes. I really enjoy his work, and I find myself leaning towards that kind of work," Josh didn't know what he had just said, but Monet was the only Great Master that came to his mind.

"That's so exciting. He is one of my favourites, too. The late 19th-century style was largely used by painters like Mount, Passer, Renoir, and Degas. They concentrated on the effects of light and pure colour," Lara realised she was babbling, "sorry, I'm sure you know all this anyway. I'd love to see one of your oils sometime."

Josh was at a loss for words. "Enough about art, tell me about Lara Sheffield?"

"Do you want the long version or the short version?"

"I want to know all there is to know, even if it takes a lifetime."

Lara wasn't too sure what he meant by that but began telling him about how she ended up living in Gauteng while her family lived in Knysna. Josh absorbed every word she said and watched her hands and body movements as if they were in a slow-motion picture.

"That's it in a nutshell. That's how I ended up starting my own PR and Marketing Consultancy. I have recently managed to land a huge account with JD Enterprises in Johannesburg, which will really make things happen for me."

"I've heard of JDE. Who are you dealing with there?"

"Old man Dillon. I was supposed to see his son, but the *arse* never pitched up for the appointment."

Josh choked on his beer.

"Are you all right?" Lara asked, concerned.

"Yes, sorry it went down the wrong way."

"Well, that is all there is about me. You must be doing okay for yourself," Lara said, changing the subject.

"Why do you say that?"

"Well, struggling artists don't normally buy the most expensive wine in the house or wear expensive sunglasses, so you must be terrific."

"Menu looks appetising. Are you ready to order?"

"You never answered my question," Lara said with a smirk on her face.

"I'm sorry, what was the question?" he looked up, pretending to be a bit puzzled.

"I wanted to know about your accomplishments as an artist."

"Let's not talk about me. I'd much rather hear all about the mysterious Lara."

"You say that like you already know a little about me."

"I'd really like to get to know you better. Is that a bit too forward? I'm not accustomed to dating, so if I start making an idiot of myself, please stop me!" Josh looked steadily into Lara's eyes just for an instant, wondering if he was sounding melodramatic.

"You seem sincere. That makes you of sound mind in my book."

"Glad to hear it."

As he said that, Lara couldn't shake the feeling that she had seen him somewhere before; he reminded her of someone. She couldn't quite put her finger on it. The hours that followed brought them closer together. She felt like she had known him for years, and she sensed that he felt the same. When the afternoon ended, and just as before, he promised to contact her but never gave a number where she could call him. Lara didn't think it was strange and put it down to him being old-fashioned. *I like it!* She thought, smiling from ear to ear. This time, she made sure she gave him her mobile phone number.

Chapter 8

Ryan had tried all day to get hold of Lara. After the last conversation, he wasn't sure she was going to respond positively to his suggestion of dinner. He knew that he had overstepped the mark more than a little this time. He wasn't proud of it either.

Persistence went hand in hand where Ryan was concerned. The eight-year affair with Lara was held together by love and passion, but mostly endurance. It was very much like a marriage, only harder. There was no commitment, no rules, and, worst of all, no guarantees. Most people would say that this was heaven. Not when you're in love. It's out of control, and there is no beginning, no end, just a middle going in circles. Ryan suddenly felt concerned. He was losing the only thing that made any sense. Lara! Ryan grabbed the telephone and dialled Lara's number. The call went to voice mail, and her gentle voice sounded out an official message.

"Hi, it's me, babes. I hope you had a successful trip. I miss you. Meet me for a drink later at the Keg, say five-thirty? Ciao!" He wasn't going to take no for an answer or give her a chance to back out. He made no mention of confirming. He knew she would never let him down.

The flight home was comfortable. Lara's frame of mind made everything a fraction more bearable. 'Jade' had phoned to say goodbye. He had said something about calling when he got back. She wasn't at all sure where he was going but was convinced that he would phone.

The traffic was heavy, and it seemed to take longer to get home from the airport than it did flying from Knysna to Joburg. She arrived home, unlocked the front door and dropped her suitcases in the entrance hall. Lara headed straight for her office, stopping only to kick her heels off. She unpacked her laptop and booted it up. She poured a glass of wine and checked her phone messages, then emails. She had received an email from JD Enterprises. It was from Peter Patterson inviting her to a cocktail party at JDE. He also apologised for emailing, explaining that he wanted to be sure she received the invitation in time. Joseph Dillon had insisted she be there. Lara smiled; she really liked the old man, and naturally, she would not miss the opportunity of meeting the 'asshole' son. There were seven messages, mostly business, with the exception of one or two friends calling and one from Ryan. Lara was disappointed that he had only left one. He obviously didn't miss her that much. She glanced at her watch; it was just five o'clock. *Time for a quick shower!*

Ryan was sitting at a table in the Keg with a window that faced the car park. He saw Lara arriving; she was late, which was unusual for her, so she must have just got in. She looked beautiful as always. Her hair was pulled up into a twist, with wisps of hair falling comfortably around her tanned face. She was wearing blue jeans, a white T-shirt, and a black linen jacket. She walked into the Keg with confidence, and Ryan watched as the heads turned. He felt a twinge in his loins; he stood up and gently kissed her on her lips. Their eyes locked on each other. It was in that second that he knew that there was something different about her.

"You look great! I ordered a bottle of wine."

"Thanks, I need it; I'm kind of pooped, to say the least."

"Good trip? Family well?"

"All fine; Robert is thrilled with the progress."

"I'm sorry about the other night."

"Save it, Ryan. I really don't want to have this conversation!"

"Sorry."

"Actually, I do think we need to talk."

"What about?"

"Us, you, me, this relationship."

"Here we go again."

"No, Ryan, you are not going to put me off that easily. I cannot go on with this emotional roller coaster anymore."

"Your sister has been talking shit into your ears again."

"This has nothing to do with Stacey."

"What then? Every time you go down there, you come back fighting."

"Not this time. We have spent too much time going nowhere, and frankly, I'm tired of it."

"What must I do? You know I can't let my wife take half of what I spent years building up. What would my kids say? You know I love you. I don't love her, you know that."

"I've heard that a million times, Ryan, but what do you want from me? You won't give either of us up. It's not right. I love you, Ryan, and I always will. But life must go on. Mine must go on with someone that will love me full time, not now and then."

"It's not like that, and you know it."

"Okay, what's to become of us, Ryan?"

Ryan pinched his lower lip with his thumb and middle finger. Lara had seen him do that so often over the years.

"You tell me? I can't stop you from living your life."

"Oh, but you do!"

"How? You are free to do what you want."

"Really, can I date other men?"

"You have in the past."

"Yes, I've gone on dates, either to make you jealous or to try and move on when we have broken up."

"I never stopped you."

"You never allowed me the room to do anything but fall back into your arms."

"Has it been all bad?"

"I love you, Ryan, and that will never change."

"Lara, I don't want to hear this."

"I met someone else."

"What!" Ryan sat up straight and folded his arms, "I knew there was something different about you; I thought it was the tan... Have you slept with him?"

"Ryan!"

"No, don't answer that."

"Well, I haven't, but I need some time to see if it will work."

"You're asking my permission?"

"I am asking you to understand why I am not going to see you for a while."

"I can't sit here and listen to this shit anymore. Are we going for dinner or not?"

Lara looked at him, "You haven't heard a word I have said."

"Let's get out of here."

Lara shook her head, snatched up her bag and followed him out the door. "Ryan... wait. I need you to say it's okay. Please help me with this."

"Are you serious about this?"

"Yes."

"Fine... I'm out of here!" Ryan waved his hands in the air as if he had just washed his hands of the subject. He got in his car and sped off, the engine screaming as he left the car park.

Just then, a waitress hurried to the door, holding an ice bucket and a bottle of wine, looking intently at Lara. "Sorry. We won't be needing that anymore." Lara said quietly.

Lara drove slowly home, thinking that even if nothing ever came of her meeting 'Jade', she had done the right thing. Ryan was her lifeline for so many years. *Let's hope you haven't cut your only air supply off!* She got home and went straight to bed. Lara lay mulling the events over until she fell asleep.

Lara woke early after a surprisingly good night's sleep. She felt somehow elated. After a quick shower, she pulled on her jeans and tied her hair up away from her face. She applied moisturiser to her face and neck, aiming for a makeup-free day. She made herself a strong cup of black coffee and curled up on the couch with JDE's 'About Us' manual. Before long, her mind was reeling with new innovative marketing ideas, and she vigorously jotted down notes. Lara spent her time pulling her ideas apart, rearranging, discarding, adding in, scribbling circles around brilliant points, and removing the not-so-good ones. By the time Lara looked up and took a break, the best part of the day had passed. She thought it odd that her mobile phone had not rung all day and she realised she had put it on silent before she went to bed. She was grateful there were no interruptions as she had really made headway with the start of her presentation.

Her mind began to wander to Ryan. Was he okay, and did he understand that this time, she was serious? He was now her past, and hopefully, Jade was her future. *Hmmm, wishful thinking perhaps*, she thought as she got up, stretched and walked to the kitchen, where she made herself another cup of coffee and a salami and mozzarella toasted sandwich. She was pretty hungry, as she had not eaten since she landed back in Joburg. She was about to pick up her phone to see if she could get hold of Stacey when the phone rang.

"You home, sweetie?"

"Stace, hi… must be mental telepathy. I was just thinking that I should phone you."

"How are you? Just checking to make sure you are safe."

"Yep, safe and sound. You'll be happy to hear that I ended things with Ryan once and for all."

"Yeah – well done. Boy, you must be really smitten with this other chap, hey?" Stacey laughed.

"You got that right, but be it Jade or not, it is time to move on."

They chatted for a while longer, and Lara got back to her presentation. She was distracted and wondered what Jade was doing. She had not heard from Ryan at all. It was a good thing for all of them, but she still felt sad. She loved him and would always have a place in her heart for him.

Lunch with Lara had gone on longer than expected, and Josh almost missed his flight to Canada. The flights were delayed, which gave him little time to prepare for the conference. The days that followed moved at a furious pace. It was dull to the end, although positive for the cash flow of JDE and its shareholders. Josh loved to travel. The romance of the European cities, especially places like Paris, Venice and Athens, was alluring. But should he be given a choice? Small tropical islands, translucent seas, and vacant white sandy beaches made for the perfect break? He thought about Lara and wondered what it would be like to make love to her, surrounded by palm trees and a warm tropical breeze. Josh had not spoken to Lara in three days. Josh's mobile rang. He checked the number and saw it was his dad. His mind quickly turned to the debacle around the accountant with sticky fingers.

"Hello."

"Josh, my boy," Joseph chirped, "how's the conference going?"

"Normal crap – this time it is particularly tedious – statistics, numbers and more stats."

"Sounds exhilarating." They both laughed.

"How are you?" Josh asked his father.

"Exhausted, but fine."

"Any more news about Blake?"

"They have still not found him and believe he is out of the country. We all have received odd phone calls, mostly hang-ups. They are all a bit spooked, and Saul seems to think it is Blake."

"Have they spoken to the Police?"

"To report what?"

"I guess that is true. Listen, Dad, I'll call you tomorrow. I have a dinner date with some of my old professors in half an hour. We can catch up then."

"No problem – chat soon."

"Thanks, Dad, bye."

"Bye, Son."

Josh hung up the phone and began to dial Lara but changed his mind. He did not have time to chat, so he decided against it. *Good things should not be rushed* – he smiled and walked into the hotel bar, "Bonjour Pierre!"

"Josh bonjour, content de te voir mon ami," Josh's professor stood up and shook his hand.

"Good to see you, Pierre. So what are we drinking?"

"Autant que possible," Pierre answered, laughing.

"As much as possible, then!" Josh said. He was sure this was going to be a long, interesting reunion.

Josh's flight back to South Africa was smooth and uneventful. He was pleased with his lecture, and his professors loved his concept. He was also grateful that it was only an annual conference. He read through the agreement that the overseas buyer was set to sign and made some changes. He sipped on a glass of red wine and picked at his meal. Aeroplane food wasn't at the top of his culinary list. The air hostess cleared away his tray, and Josh began to relax. His thoughts turned to Lara. He still had not contacted her, nor had he told her that he had a home in Johannesburg and basically only spent his weekends fishing in Knysna. When he thought about it, he had not told her much, and what he told her was mostly a lie. He started to wonder if he should cut his losses and not call her again. *Hell no!* That thought quickly passed. He planned to call her as soon as he was cleared through customs. And that is precisely what he did.

"Lara honey, it's Josh, I mean Jade."

"Confused about your identity today, are you?" she laughed.

"More than you know," he replied, knowing that was at least honest, "I'm in Johannesburg this week and thought we could get together."

"When?" as she said it, she winced, regretting sounding desperate, "Ah yes, I mean sure, anytime."

"Well, are you free for lunch today?"

"Sure, what time and where?"

"Dime & Thyme in Rosebank say twelve-twenty, or I can come pick you up?"

"No, no, not to worry. I have some shopping to do and will meet you there."

They said their goodbyes, leaving Josh happy that she was not that upset that he had not called. That made her more attractive.

Josh had promised to catch up with his dad, so he went directly to the office. There was no more news about the Blake saga, and they all seemed uninterested in wasting much more time on it. It was a criminal case, and the Police would have to solve it. They had other business at hand. Josh, however, did alert security at the building that Blake had jumped bail and that security should be increased. Passwords, keys, etc., had been changed already, so they felt certain he was locked out of the business and building.

Josh arrived at the restaurant to find Lara waiting at the bar. He walked up to her, smiling.

"Hey, you. Sorry I'm a bit late," he whispered as he kissed her gently on her cheek.

Lara smiled with a surprised look on her face, her eyes quickly looking him up and down.

"Did someone die?" Lara quizzed Josh, looking surprised, "What's with the suit and tie?"

Josh almost choked, not prepared for the question, "Um, what, the suit? Oh, yeah. Had a meeting," he tried to look sincere but felt like a heel. "Why? Don't you approve?" he asked, looking hurt.

"Hell yes, I think you look dreadfully handsome and not at all like a struggling artist," Lara said playfully. "How are you, Jade?'

"Actually, a whole lot better now that I'm with you, Lara," Josh pulled up a vacant bar stool and sat next to Lara.

"I took the liberty of ordering a bottle of wine. I hope that's okay."

"Lovely," Josh said, signalling the bartender, "another glass please."

The barman poured a glass for Josh and topped up Lara's.

"Your table is ready when you are, Sir."

"Thanks – just give us a moment," he turned to Lara. She was looking as beautiful as ever. She had a gentle, loving look in her eyes. Josh decided then, no more lies. He had to tell her the truth.

"Lara, I must tell you something. Actually, it's more of a confession."

"Wow, this does sound serious. Please don't tell me you are married?" she said, teasing him. He smiled and gently touched her chin.

"No, nothing like that," he paused and sipped his wine, but before he could continue, Lara interrupted him.

"Hold that thought; our table is ready," she said, pointing to the waiter waiting to seat them, "and I need the loo… I'll meet you at the table, and we can continue this confession hour," she said with a wave, gracefully meandering through the tables.

Lara made light of it, and although she did not know 'Jade' very well, she picked up that he was more than serious about what he had to say. Lara needed to collect her thoughts and wanted to be prepared for whatever was about to be confessed. *Think good thoughts, Lara. The only thing that would really irk you is lying, so breathe and relax.* Lara had always detested lies; she had never seen the need for them. Taking your punishment and telling the truth was what she always believed. She was convinced 'Jade' had absolutely no reason to lie to her. Although she was now curious. *We all know what that did to the cat!*

"Your table is this way, Sir,' the waiter announced, ushering Josh through the tables. The table that was set aside for them was positioned in a cosy yet sunny corner of the restaurant. They had a stunning view looking onto a secluded Zen Garden with glorious little bridges winding over a Koi Pond.

"Thank you – please see that my guest finds her way here," Josh said, and with that, his mobile phone rang. It was Saul, "Saul, what's up?"

"Josh. Sorry to worry you, but I have just had a call from Sherman, and he is pretty pissed off."

"More than usual?" Josh said, laughing. 'What now?"

"He is going on about the buyers we lined up for him and wants to meet this afternoon at three."

"Shouldn't be a problem. Do me a favour. Call him back to see if you can push it out to three-thirty. Also, let him know that I have spoken to the local buyers as well as the overseas prospects. They are good to go. I spoke to Tokyo this morning; the agreement was signed and should have been emailed to my office by now. I believe the architect's plans were delivered this morning. Check with Mrs P…" Josh didn't complete the sentence; Lara was standing staring, wide-eyed, with a little puzzled look on her face. "Saul set it up. I'll be there. And let me know if you have any problems. Got to go. Ciao," he hung up, simultaneously standing up to pull a chair out for Lara. He wasn't sure what or how much she had heard of his conversation, although the look on her face gave him reason to believe it was enough. *Oh boy*! He smiled at her and cleared his throat, "Would you like some more wine before we order?"

"Artist, my arse! Jade, what is going on? I heard more than enough to know that you may paint as a hobby, but it's not what you do for a living, is it?"

"Lara - I," he tried to interrupt.

"No, Jade! Why are you lying about being an artist when clearly you are not? The suit, expensive taste – now the phone call – it all makes sense now,' she sounded hurt and anxious. *Oh, shit, it had to be a lie!*

"Lara… honey."

"Please don't call me honey; just answer my questions."

"I am trying to. If you would just calm down and let me talk."

"Oh, I'm all ears and this better be good," Lara said, folding her arms while leaning back in her chair.

"As I arrived today and before you went to the lady's room, I said I had a confession to make. Well, I wanted to tell you that I misled you unintentionally when we first met. I am not an artist; you are right about that. Couldn't paint a flat wall, to be perfectly honest."

Lara stared at him, frowning.

"There is more. My name is not Jade. It is Josh. My friends call me JD," he said as calmly as he could, hoping it sounded like no big deal.

Lara was really frowning now. Josh watched her cheeks turn crimson. *She's getting angry,* he thought.

"What, I don't understand, why did you lie?"

"I didn't exactly lie about my name. When you asked me what my name was, I said JD, and you mistook it for Jade. The telephone line was not that clear, and I didn't correct you," he hesitated and said, "For what reason, I'm not really sure."

"The artist story, did I mistake that too?"

"No, that was my doing, for which I sincerely apologise," Josh tried to put on his best puppy dog look and continued, "and it was more about self-preservation than anything else."

"What is that supposed to mean?"

"I'm a businessman; successful, wealthy… and in the past have met some people that have used me for their own objectives, which has made me wary, and I suspect, distrusting. I did not want it to influence you one way or another."

He took one look at the disgust on her face. "That's my mistake, I know. I didn't want to sway you – shit, this is coming out all wrong. Believe me, Lara. It seemed the right thing to do at the time. Clearly, it was not."

Lara let out a sigh. "You pretentious ass, you know nothing about me, yet you chose to manipulate this relationship from the start."

"Believe me when I say it was not like that. I'm accustomed to meeting people who are attracted to my status rather than the person – does that make any sense at all?" He continued quickly as she was getting ready to leave. "Lara, when I met you, I knew that I did not want this to be like the other women I met. I wanted to make sure it didn't matter to you who or what I did. Is that so wrong?"

"Right now, I don't know what to think. I'm not sure what kind of people or women you have dated or been associated with in the past that have dragged you to this point, but where I come from, honesty and loyalty are our priorities. I would have hoped that it was transparent when you met me," she huffed, picked up her bag and began to leave. Josh grabbed her arm.

"Please don't leave – I'm truly sorry – it was a ridiculous thing to do."

"Jade, Josh, whoever the hell you are, when you make up your mind, call me. Right now, I really have no interest in your bullshit." She continued in a steady tone, "Relationships are built on trust. How can there be friendship or love without trust – think about that and your bloody preservation theory!"

Before Josh released his hold on her, he said, "There is more I need to tell you. Please stay and let me finish."

Lara gave him a dirty look, "I think I have heard enough for one day."

"Lara, please let me finish," he watched as she strutted out of the restaurant. *Nice work, Josh. She is right, you are an ass. You really have some serious tap-dancing to do to make up for this.* Then Josh thought of something else: *wait until she finds out I'm her new boss.* Josh paid the bill and left. Before heading back to the office, he made one especially important stop.

Lara was really confused about what had just transpired. *Was this man for real? Why was he playing games? What was he hiding? He seemed genuine in his apology and explanation. Obviously, there was much more to this saga than he was letting on. Am I wrong about him, and is he really an egotistical ass?* Her mind was racing.

Lara arrived at home feeling overwhelmed and disappointed. She made a cup of coffee and a sandwich. Lunch was a disaster, and she'd eaten nothing else during the day. Her thoughts went to Dillion Enterprises. *I can't deal with Josh right now, what with less than a week to the second meeting. I need to focus on my presentation. This will have to wait until I'm done.*

She sat in front of her laptop and began working on her presentation. She was excited about how her presentation was coming together. She spent most of the day engrossed in what she was doing. She had done this all her working life and knew when her ideas would 'wow' her audience. She was positive this was going to be one of those times.

She had received an email from Joseph, who let her know that they had some publicity problems. He stressed that her job had become more important than before. Public relations were at an all-time low, and he would appreciate her concentrating on that aspect of JDE's corporate identity transformation. The doorbell chimed, giving Lara a jolt. She walked over and peered through the peephole; it was a florist. She opened the door.

"Lara Sheffield?" asked the young lady.

"Yes," Lara stared at what looked like fifty or so red roses in a stunning crystal vase. She thanked the florist, closed the door, and looked for a card. It simply read, 'Forgive an ass who never meant to mislead or hurt you in any way. Josh.'

Lara smiled and shrugged her shoulders. *All in good time, Jade – I mean Josh*. It suddenly occurred to her that Smith might not be his surname. She leaned in to smell the roses and placed the gorgeous bouquet on the coffee table. She returned to her desk and typed away with a little more confidence, pausing only to glance up at the roses.

CHAPTER 9

Josh did not try to call Lara but hoped that the roses would make up a little for the lies told past, present and future. He still had to tell her about JDE. There was so much on the go, but he also knew that Lara would be seeing him sooner than she realised at the planned meeting at JDE, which was set for the following week. He knew that he had to tell her that he was Joshua Dillon. He had to talk to her before then! He had no intentions of blowing her presentation or embarrassing her in front of the Board and his dad.

Josh arrived at the office at a suitable time for the meeting with Sherman. He briefly spoke to Mrs Perkins and managed to return a few calls before it began. He phoned Chantilly to check on Wrinkles. Grace was amazing at looking after his home and dog while he was in Joburg, so he knew that Wrinkles was well-fed and loved in his absence. He wanted to ask Lara to go with him to Knysna on the upcoming weekend, and by then, all would be clear and hopefully on track again. *I should phone Lara this evening and chat with her.* He made a mental note.

Josh's meeting with Sherman went well. The deal he brokered was a triumph; Sherman, for once, was a relatively happy man. The Tokyo developers would be building the hotel in conjunction with local property developers, and it was aptly named Sherman's Amusement Park and Waterfront. This was a project that was worth millions to JDE. Josh shivered at the thought that Blake could have ruined the deal by selling information to their opposition. He had really played this transaction close to his chest. In hindsight, his gut feeling was to keep it quiet. How right he had been. He wondered where on earth Blake had got to. It made him sick to his stomach to think of him on some tropical island sipping cocktails from a coconut. JDE had paid millions of Rands for it. *A very expensive coconut indeed,* he thought.

Just then, Peter walked in. "Josh… hi… got a moment to chat?"

"Sure, Pete. Let's grab a cup of coffee in my office."

"Hmm, sounds good," Peter agreed, following Josh into his office. Mrs Perkins walked in with a tray stacked with coffee and biscuits. He wondered how she did that. She must have ears and eyes in the back of her head. She was so efficient it was scary. "Thanks, Mrs Perkins, you are a honey." She merely smiled at Josh and drifted out of the office, closing the door behind her. Josh and Peter helped themselves.

"How's the party coming on?" Josh enquired.

"Most RSVPs are in, and as always, with free food and booze, most of the guests are coming," he chuckled.

"What about Lara Sheffield?"

"I spoke to her this morning; she will be there."

"Is she bringing a partner?"

"What's with the twenty questions?"

Josh laughed, "Just interested, that's all."

"She is coming alone," Peter smiled, raising an eyebrow, "you happy?"

"Yeah, don't mention this to my dad."

"Why?" Peter looked puzzled.

"Long story." Josh filled Peter in on his dad's little deception and how he met Lara. Suitably embarrassed, he also shared with him what had happened since then.

"Nice, JD – you really are an all-time romantic!" Peter couldn't hide the sarcasm in his voice. He laughed again.

"Hey, I know I stuffed up. Give me a break."

"Do you really want to see her again? On second thoughts, you don't have a choice."

"Even if she did not work for us, I would choose to be with her. She is amazing, Pete. I only hope I have not made a total fool of myself and that she will forgive me."

"Maybe you should tell her the whole truth. One mistake a person can forgive but make a habit of lying, and you are going to lose big time."

"Tell me about it – I'm going to phone her tonight."

"Don't phone; pitch up on her doorstep with flowers."

"I have done the flowers, but you are right. This all has to come out in the open."

"Good luck with that," he said.

"Thanks, something tells me I am going to need it," Josh said, rubbing his neck.

"To change the subject, I wanted to ask you what news you have heard about Blake?" Peter asked as he stood up to refill his coffee. "Do you want a refill," he said, gesturing to Josh.

"Yes, please. I spoke to the detective in charge of the case. I forget his name."

"Matsinye, Ed."

"Right, that's the chap. He said they have posted his details on international channels, but more than that, there is little they can do. They must wait for him to slip up and leave a trail."

"Do you think we have to worry? What if he is still in South Africa? Saul is a little spooked. He believes Blake is quite capable of carrying out his threat of revenge."

"There is no telling what a person is capable of when pushed into a corner. I'll talk to Saul. Let's go to the pub after work today and have a drink. I'll get my dad and Saul to join. The four of us can catch up then.

"Good idea," Peter nodded in agreement.

CHAPTER 10

Blake stood on the deck of the cabin with arms folded and eyes fixed on the dirt road. Waiting. I wondered if he had done the right thing by bringing Seth and his sidekick on board. He had to trust someone. This was not something he could do alone. His plan required intelligence, muscle and men who were hungry for a fast buck.

The Dillions had underestimated his loyalty and never gave him the credit he felt he deserved. *That's their first mistake, and the second would be to underestimate me again.* People never took accountants seriously, having that stigma as boring, old men in grey suits. *If they could see me now,* he laughed. Blake had fattened up, and with the new bald look, he was, without a doubt, a different man.

He had changed the look of the Panel Van so that it could pass for any regular maintenance vehicle. These were the first steps towards his revenge on the Dillon Empire. *Empires rise, and Empires fall, and so too do their Emperors. Soon, JDE would meet that same fate: old man Joseph, Joshua, and anyone else that got in the way.* Blake embraced the thought. The smirk on his face was affirmation.

In the distance, he saw a car travelling at a high speed, leaving a dust trail that was kilometres long. *Idiots! What part of discreetly did they not understand.* He had met Seth when they shared a holding cell the night that Blake was arrested. Seth was due to be released after spending two years in jail for a botched car theft. He wasn't the brightest fellow in the world, but Blake did not mix with any hardened criminals to speak of, so his henchman choices were limited. Time was of the essence. His new accomplice had mentioned his cousin Cliff would do anything that he told him to do. Obedient family members were key to Blake's mission. *Mission.* The word empowered him. The car drew closer and turned into the driveway of the cabin. Blake pointed to the barn, directing them to park inside, wanting to conceal any activity that could bring nosy neighbours calling. They walked up to Blake and said they were there to see Mr Henry.

Blake laughed. "Come in, and let's get acquainted. I'm Winston Van Niekerk." Blake was thrilled not to be recognised. *A truly magnificent transformation on his part*, he mused. If he ran into a person he once knew, he was confident they would not realise that Winston van Niekerk was none other than Blake Henry! Seth gave a shriek when he realised Winston was indeed his ex-cellmate.

After getting some meat on the braai and sharing a few bonding drinks, Blake gave them a rundown of what he envisaged. These men were extremely comfortable with a life of crime. The task ahead was just another well-paying job. That made them eager, and Blake was paying them very well indeed. This made them a team.

The days that followed were spent with Blake's delegating and scheming. Seth had instructions to keep JDE under constant surveillance. He would stake out JDE at various positions next to the building. He busied himself with taking photos of people entering and leaving. Each night, Blake would download the shots taken by Seth and would spend hours carefully scanning the pictures to ensure that when the time came, each piece of his puzzle would fall into place.

Of the emails Blake had managed to intercept, a few were important to his plot. JDE security was slow in changing passwords, and the filters that he had set up were still working on critical addresses. He was particularly interested in an inter-office email which Peter had distributed. He had updated staff on the official PR party that they were throwing for their clients. As always, Peter had been thorough in supplying all the necessary details. Winston now had a perfect cover. He decided to gain access to the party under the pretence of being a caterer. It was that simple. Winston had to smile. He was not heading for a life of crime, just sweet revenge. The only snag he could see was time! They had less than two weeks to coordinate each intricate part of the plan. Blake was accustomed to working with the pressure turned on. He felt exhilarated and eager to get moving.

Cliff had turned out to be a lot brighter than Blake had first suspected. He was proving to be invaluable and worth every cent that Blake was paying him. Cliff had a knack for finding the gear and equipment that they would need. He had the right connections for obtaining untraceable mobile phones and firearms, while most of the other gear they needed could be bought at local camping or Co-op stores. Nowadays, you could kit an army of mercenaries without question. However, everything still needed to be untraceable. Winston's recent lessons with the power of a paper trail meant he now insisted on cash-only deals. Cliff's understanding thereof was clear. Blake was at ease with these men, and this made him even more confident.

"Cliff! Hey, Cliff!" he shouted. "You need to get to the hardware store and get the materials we need – we have a van to prepare."

"No problem, Boss."

"Don't forget to spread your purchases over a few different stores – don't draw attention to yourself," he added.

"No worries... I will be back in a few hours. Do we need anything else?"

"Yeah, get meat for a braai. Oh, and get more beer. The rugby is on, and we all could do with a break over the weekend. There is cash on the counter."

Blake was not the sensitive type, nor was he artistic. He did, however, have exceptional computer skills, and his creativity in this regard dazzled the best in the field. They had to clone one of their vehicles and needed a template for the logo of the catering firm to do a proper job. The vehicle was not the problem, but the logo had to be accurate. Working with a good photographic programme allowed Blake the option of building an almost perfect template. Next, with a can or two of spray paint and a bit of luck, they would be in business. Blake chuckled. He had specifically chosen the catering company because they had a simple logo to copy. Their surveillance revealed that a Panel Van was the vehicle used most often by the catering company. Cliff arrived back with all the items on Blake's list. It took some tedious work, but the template worked out perfectly and soon, the Van was a reliable copy. They were all set.

Josh was up early. They had gone for drinks after work, and it had turned into a late evening. He never got a chance to phone Lara, either. After a tough workout, Josh took a hot shower. He got out and wrapped a white towel around his waist, letting the morning air dry him off while his emails downloaded. He began to dress and was busy with his tie when he stopped in his tracks. He could not stop thinking about Lara. He stared at the phone, feeling nervous about talking to her. She had not responded to the apology and flowers. That was never a good sign. He thought about sending a text message but decided that would be tacky. He dialled her number. He had butterflies in his stomach. Josh sighed, feeling like a foolish schoolboy. The phone seemed to ring for ages. Josh's hot shower was making him sweat. He heard Lara's voice and was about to say something when he heard it was her voicemail. He waited for the tone, "Lara, hi, it's Josh. We really need to talk. I am going to Knysna for the weekend and was hoping you would come with me. There are a few things we need to clear up. I will email the details and flight plan to you." Josh hung up.

Lara was sitting on the sofa with her legs crossed, nibbling on her thumbnail, listening intently to the message Josh was leaving. Part of her wanted to jump up and call him back; the other part wanted never to speak to him again. The thought of going to Knysna was appealing as she could see Stacey. It wasn't so much Josh that was the problem but her presentation to JDE that was foremost on her mind. She stood up and went to check her email. The flight plan was there, as promised. She was a little surprised that he had a company jet at his disposal, and that intrigued her even more. *Who is this guy?* Although she was disappointed, she knew it was not a clever idea.

It was bad timing, and she did not want anything to jeopardise her shot at working for one of the largest property conglomerates in the world. She quickly answered the email with a polite 'thank you for the invite' and let him know that she was away and would not be able to take him up on his offer. She also made it clear that she was not contactable and would phone him the following week, and they could chat then. She sent the mail off and made a note to call him after her meeting with JDE.

Josh was finishing off his coffee when he heard his computer chime – he had mail. Checking his messages, he was surprised to see that Lara had responded so quickly. Had she been at home when he called, he wondered. She not only declined his offer, but he was not going to see her before the meeting. *This was going from upsetting to horrendous*, Josh thought, grimacing. He had to tell her face-to-face or at least on the telephone that he was Joshua Dillon before her presentation. He did not want to rattle her before she presented to the Board. Josh would have to come up with a decent plan.

CHAPTER 11

Mrs Perkins arrived earlier than usual. She prided herself on her organisational skills. She wanted to ensure she would be well prepared for the day's events. Lara Sheffield would be back to meet with the Board. She needed to make sure all the necessary arrangements were made for her presentation. Refreshments would have to be served on arrival, with a light lunch arranged before departure. She made a mental note to give Josh a call to remind him. His father had made a point of telling her to make sure he was there.

Lara had decided to get to her appointment early to ensure that her laptop was compatible with their equipment. She wanted everything to go off without a hitch. She was excited and not the least bit nervous. She had gone over and over her presentation numerous times throughout the weekend. Mrs Perkins had turned out to be remarkably helpful and surprisingly pleasant. They gelled together. They even had a few things in common. Mrs Perkins picked up on her confidence and enthusiasm and knew Lara was there with purpose and skill.

Peter was the first to arrive, greeting Mrs Perkins with a grin and a white rose he had swiped from the foyer's display. Lara smiled at his tenacity. He acknowledged her with the same gusto and charm he had greeting Mrs Perkins. He had a look in his green eyes that said he knew something about her that she didn't know herself. *How odd,* thought Lara, but let it pass as she held her nerve for the presentation.

Before long, the Board members had arrived, and with composure and style, Joseph arrived. Lara's nerves wavered ever so slightly. Joseph had that aura about him. He had a commanding presence that few men did, and others dreamed of. Lara's thoughts turned to Josh. She quickly pushed him to the back of her mind, annoyed that she had let her mind wander to her personal life. She turned and focused on the man standing in front of her. She was busy chatting with Saul Gerber when she noticed that Joseph was irritated while in conversation with Mrs Perkins. She saw him shaking his head. He was phoning someone, and by the look on his face, he was not having any luck getting through. He muttered something to Mrs Perkins and turned to everyone, "People, let's get the show on the road. It would appear my son is going to be late," he walked over to Lara and continued, "My apologies, my dear but we will start without him." Lara was not in the least worried as she had never met him and was eager to get things underway.

Josh stood in the foyer of JDE, ignoring his mobile phone. Mrs Perkins had called; his father had called; even Peter had tried to track him down. Josh had gone into hiding for the moment. He wanted Lara to get through her presentation without interference. He planned to sneak in when the lights were low – she would not even know that he was there. He really did want to see what she could do for the company, and in truth, he was anxious to see her again.

Lara began with a brief introductory summary of what she had intended to reveal. She stood in the proper position, chin up, shoulders back, oozing confidence – her sincerity and skill clear, and her proposal unrivalled. She was so engrossed with her presentation that she hardly noticed the captive audience staring back at her. The person who had entered late was even overlooked. Josh stood quietly in the dark at the back of the Boardroom. Josh's entrance did not go totally unnoticed by his father. Joseph gave his son one of his disgruntled nods before returning his attention to Lara.

Josh watched Lara progress through her presentation with confidence. Josh was in awe of her aptitude and grace. He began to feel unbelievably guilty and more anxious as to the outcome of today's reveal. He continued to hang on her every word. Lara stood silently while her multimedia presentation ran its course. Josh couldn't take his eyes off her, and for a minute, he thought their eyes made contact. It shook him for a minute, and he realised, thankfully, that she could not see him.

When the presentation came to its conclusion, Saul turned the lights up. The Board applauded Lara's efforts. Josh was one of them. Lara had a gorgeous smile on her face as she glanced, thanking everyone individually with a curt nod of her head. As she focused on Josh standing in the back, her smile receded, and her eyes grew a little wider. The confused look on her face quickly diminished as she concentrated on what Joseph was saying.

"Well done, Lara! That was superb."

"Thank you, Joseph," Lara was pleased with herself but, for the life of her, did not know why Josh was standing there. She couldn't help but stare at him. Joseph picked up on Lara's intrigue.

"Lara Sheffield, I would like you to meet Joshua Dillon, our MD, and my very tardy son. Josh, *this* is Lara."

"Lara – very nice to finally meet you. I enjoyed your presentation immensely," Josh said, shaking her hand. He could see Lara was speechless, so he quickly continued, "I hope you will forgive me for my late arrival." He watched Lara's cheekbones turn rosy. She was not blushing. He suddenly felt nervous.

"No problem, Joshua – it is good to finally put a name to the face," Lara smirked. Josh glanced at his father. The remark appeared to go unnoticed by Joseph.

"Yes, my dear, the prodigal son has returned," Joseph said, laughing, "please come… let's have some refreshments before we continue our meeting."

Lara was grateful no one picked up on her snide remark and was thrilled it made Josh squirm. She was bursting with questions and could not believe what was happening. Josh was Joshua Dillon. The Joshua Dillion. She guessed that that was what he wanted to tell her. She couldn't help but feel foolish and duped by him once again. She could feel Josh staring at her; she glanced his way. He had a worried, boyish grin on his face. He walked up to her, handing her a cup of coffee. She managed to take it from him without spilling. Her hands were shaking.

"It is really good to see you, Lara."

"I have to say I was very surprised to see you, Josh, anything else I should know?"

"Yes, there is a lot you need to know. Most important is how sorry I am and that I care deeply about you."

"I don't think this is the place or time, Josh," she cut him short, "there are a few things we do need to discuss, just not here and not now, please. This is genuinely important to me, and I must focus."

"Of course, I understand. Will you have dinner with me tonight?"

"Yes," Lara answered as Joseph joined them.

"I see you are getting acquainted with our lovely Lara, Josh."

"Yes, Dad, and you did not do her justice. She is breathtaking."

Lara was feeling awkward, mustering only a smile. He saw the surprised look on his father's face. She desperately needed to collect herself and politely excused herself, asking where the lady's bathroom was situated. Two minutes later, she received a text message on her mobile phone. It was Josh. *I'll pick you up at six-thirty – looking forward to it.* Lara smiled; she was looking forward to it more than she cared to admit. Lara had reason to celebrate. She entered the first significant contract of her career and was ecstatic.

The rest of the afternoon was spent with Lara and Josh, now working side by side, together with the Board members. Issues at hand were dealt with. They covered all the suggestions that Lara had outlined in her proposal. Mrs Perkins dutifully took the minutes, each attendee having matters on hand to deal with. Lara was now privy to them. Meeting dates were set, business cards exchanged, and the chemistry was explosive. Joseph was pleased with the results and the tremendous energy that surged throughout the meeting. He was intrigued by the chemistry between Josh and Lara. He couldn't shake the feeling that he was missing something. He put it down to him, fooling Josh into believing Lara was less than 'breath-taking' as Josh put it. An inappropriate comment for one's first meeting, he thought.

Lara left the meeting tired but overjoyed. She spent what little time she had left in the day putting her family in the picture. They were thrilled and proud of what she accomplished. Exciting days lay ahead. There was a tingle of anticipation at the prospect of having dinner with one of the most powerful men in the country. It dawned on her that Josh was her new boss. A man who pulled the wool over her eyes. A combination she had trouble comprehending. Lara took a leisurely bubble bath and pondered on what she would wear. She tried on a few different outfits and settled on black pants and a shoestring-strapped, raw silk top. Lara added a touch of sparkle for the evening. She completed her look with a delicate gold chain and a pair of diamond earrings. Her makeup was a little heavier than she would typically apply during the day. The charcoal eyeshadow gave her blue eyes a sensual, smoky look. She could wear high heels as Josh would still tower over her. Just as in the morning, her perfume was subtle – different, but just as subtle. A glass bottle of liquid gold. A must for any woman.

Josh was punctual and arrived with a massive bunch of Tiger Lilies. He took a little gasp when Lara opened the door. She stood there looking like an angel. Her blue eyes were smouldering but on guard. He had never seen her like this and thought that he had never seen anything more exquisite.
"Hi."
"Hi."

Josh handed her the flowers, and she smiled, ushering him in. Josh took a curt bow and walked in. He could not help what he did next. Lara closed the door, and as she turned, Josh pulled her into his arms. He placed his hand gently on the nape of her neck, holding her still while he firmly kissed her, gently earning the respect of her lips. Josh felt her arms fall to her side as she succumbed to his resolve. As quickly as he had set the kiss in motion, he gently pulled away. When she finally opened her eyes, he was staring into them. Lara felt weak and astonished.

"I better give these some more… I mean water," holding the flowers, she drifted to the kitchen. Josh took a deep breath and cupped his mouth like he was savouring the moment. That was the hardest thing he had done in years. He could have kissed her all night. He had forgotten that warm sensation that engulfs one in a moment such as that. He smiled as Lara appeared looking bemused.

"Can I get you something to drink?"

"I think we should get going. We have reservations."

"Yes, well, let me get my bag… won't be a moment."

"No problem. I'm not going anywhere without you," Josh said gently, adding, "Ever." Lara's head swung around, and she looked at him for a moment. She picked up her bag, and with that, they headed off, side by side, almost glad, almost comfortable, almost there.

Joseph was pleased with the outcome of the day's events and had asked Saul, Peter, and Josh out for dinner. Josh declined without a hint of what he had to do that was better than a good steak and a full-bodied Cabernet. He knew his son only too well and guessed it was a full-bodied woman who was more interesting than a night out with the boys. He couldn't help wondering who he was seeing. Lara Sheffield popped into his mind, but he quickly brushed it off. *Not even Josh could work that fast,* he chuckled to himself. Joseph was the last to arrive. Peter and Saul were sitting at the pub waiting for him.

"Gentleman, I see you started without me," he said, laughing.

"You're late, my friend and time is a wasting," cheered Saul.

"What can we get you?"

"Peter, my boy, as much as possible," he said, patting him on the shoulder, "but for now, a draft with my thanks."

"Josh not joining us?" Saul asked.

"Hmm, no, I think he has a date."

"When has Josh not got a date?" Peter added, laughing as he handed Joseph his beer.

"All my life, I longed for someone to say that about me!" Saul groaned.

"Hey, I remember you had your share of women swooning over you."

"Hell yeah, that was when I had a six-pack and not a keg," they all roared with laughter.

"Well, I hope you will fit into your Tux for Friday?"

"Pete, you are not serious… Black Tie?"

Peter sighed, "Don't you people read your emails?" he said, throwing his hands in the air.

"Don't panic, Saul, do what I do, hire the damn thing," Joseph sipped his beer.

"Looks like I will have to hire one – nothing fits anymore," Saul mumbled.

"So, what do you think of our Ms Sheffield?"

"Hmmm. A looker, that one."

Peter added, "Nice boobs."

"Actually, I was talking about her presentation," Joseph shrieked with laughter. Peter and Saul's laughter filled the pub. Joseph continued, "The chemistry between my son and her was explosive. How weird was that? Looked like they have known each other for years."

Saul responded, "Yeah, I noticed that too."

"Well, you know Josh, he is an easy chap to get on with," Peter tried to sound convincing.

"Nah! There were sparks flying between those two," Joseph continued the debate on the chemistry between men and women. They were so engrossed in their 'attraction' discussion that they were oblivious to their surroundings.

The bar had filled with the buzz of chatter and comfortable laughter. Blake stood at the entrance, eyes squinting, as he tried to focus on the faces throughout the busy pub. He paused for a moment, staring at the people sitting around the bar. He grinned. He was particularly interested in the three men seated at the far end of the bar counter, JDE's Board members enjoying a social get-together. Surprisingly enough, he was not even nervous but rather confident that he would go unrecognised. He chuckled to himself. A few months ago, he would have been one of the trusted employees drinking with the great Joseph Dillon. Blake made his way to the bar with confidence. He chose a bar stool next to Saul.

"Excuse me… is this chair taken?" he said in a guttural German accent.

Saul turned and looked directly at Blake, "No, you are welcome to it." Saul turned away without a second glance. Blake tipped his hat at Peter and Joseph. He felt a rush of adrenalin. Not one of them had given him a second glance. He ordered a beer and drank leisurely, listening to every word spoken between the three men.

The candlelight flickered bewitchingly, lighting up the crystal wine goblets. Eyes fixed on one another, both waiting for the other to break the melodious silence. Josh drew a deep breath. He knew the lead was his to take. He took her hand, cupping it between his. Then, he gently lifted her hand, turning it slowly, kissing the centre of her palm.

"You were magnificent today."

"So you said Josh twice in the car on our way here," Lara said, removing her hand, letting just the tip of her finger linger under his chin for a moment.

"Sorry."

"No, don't apologise. I appreciate all the applause I can get."

"Lara... not to make another apology, but I am truly regretting the fact I was not straight up with you. There is no excuse. I hurt you and..."

"Josh, let it go. I really am not going to punish you anymore for this. Yes, you did misrepresent yourself, but that is over now," Lara paused as the waiter replenished their wine, "I'm prepared to move on if you are. There is so much I really don't know about you; I have so many questions. So, it is your turn – the truth about Joshua Dillon and let the rest go."

Josh let out a huge sigh. "You are a remarkable woman, and I'm a very lucky man."

"The truth is all I ask for. Suffice it to say, don't lie to me again. Ever. I do have to add that should there be a next time you are not honest with me, there won't be a next time for us," Lara said with a serious look on her face.

"Yeah, and that is fair, very fair."

"Good. Enough gloom. Let's get back to basics… and eat because I'm starving!" Lara chimed while she opened the menu.

Josh picked up his menu, relieved that Lara had been gracious about the whole saga. They chatted about the various dishes on offer…their likes, and dislikes. Soon, the hum of voices and flurry of patrons in the restaurant faded away, leaving Josh and Lara in a world of their own, surrounded by the candlelight while shadows danced gracefully around them.

Lara was pleasantly surprised at how the evening had turned out. Lara realised that he was the man she had met on the beach in Brenton-on-Sea, gentle and compassionate, witty and smart. Lara felt good about herself, which was a forgotten and extraordinary feeling.

"You're smiling. Was it something I said?"

"No, I was just thinking. I'm glad we had dinner tonight," Lara said, pushing her hair over her shoulder.

"Well, pretty lady, not as glad as I am. Would it be presumptuous of me if I asked you to go with me to JDE's cocktail party?" Josh asked Lara.

"There's no one I'd rather go with…" Lara whispered, looking intently at Josh. "Would there be a problem with us going on a date and working together?"

"Not with me," Josh said cheerfully.

"You know that I was referring to your dad, amongst others."

"We do have a strict policy of no office romances between employees."

"Oh."

"Good thing you are not an employee, and neither am I," Josh laughed.

"Ooh, funny man… seriously though, what will they say?"

"Who cares! There will be loads of people there. No one will be bothered, so don't worry."

"Okay. Good. Now I just need to find a gown to wear," Lara said, "I believe the dress code is 'Formal'."

"I guess I'll need to dust the old Tux off. I'll pick you up at seven on Friday evening, then?"

Lara smiled, "Yeah, thanks, that's perfect."

"What size do you wear."

"Josh! Why have you got a spare Tux for me?" they both laughed.

"C'mon Lara, humour me, please."

"Normally, a size 34 – happy?"

"Very. Feel like an Irish coffee?"

"Don Pedro, rather, thanks."

Josh called the waiter over, "The bill, please."

"Hey, what about my Don Pedro?"

"No problem, I've got ice cream and whisky at home," Josh said with a smirk on his face. Lara chuckled nervously.

Josh had hoped his dad was asleep. He wanted to avoid having to explain why Lara was at the house. He could not resist taking her home, wanting desperately to get her alone. They arrived at the Estate, and Josh could see that Lara was impressed. He loved her gasps of delight at the size of their home, which was surrounded by spectacular gardens. Josh led her through the foyer towards the kitchen. Joseph was nowhere to be seen. He breathed a sigh of relief.

"Make yourself at home and let me work my magic."

"Hmm, sounds wonderful… do you mind?" Lara said, pointing at the photos on the sideboard.

"Nah, go ahead, mainly family pics."

"Who's the babe?" Lara said, holding up an antique silver frame.

"My mom," Josh answered with a laugh.

"Wow, she is beautiful."

The sound of the blender rang through the air, and Lara wandered off to do a scenic tour of the house. She loved the idea of snooping, taking in the absolute luxury of the place. She stepped out onto the patio; her mouth dropped open. The swimming pool was exquisitely set amongst different-sized boulders. It was one of the better rock pools she had seen, beautifully lit up with thoughtfully placed mood lights. A waterfall flowed into a smaller pool, which in turn overflowed into the main pool. It was glorious. Lara looked back into the house to check on Josh. She could see that he was still busy with the drinks. She giggled and began to take her clothes off.

"Perhaps I should leave."

"Aaah!" Lara screamed, quickly covering up. Lara spun around quickly. She had not seen Joseph lying on a sun bed in the dark of the patio.

"I did not mean to startle you, my dear."

"Joseph, hi – I did not see you there," Lara stammered.

"I must have nodded off," Joseph yawned. "So, you are Josh's mysterious date."

"Yes, I'm afraid that would be me."

"Nothing to be afraid of. Two good people getting together is a damn fine idea to me." Joseph stood up and looked at Lara, "If my son does not treat you right, let me know."

"Oh – Dad, you're up. Don Pedro?" Josh said, grinning, holding up the glasses.

"That looks like a chocolate milkshake."

"Hmm, yeah, we only had chocolate ice cream," Josh frowned, and they all laughed.

"Not tonight. I will leave you in peace," Joseph stood up, "Lovely to see you again, Lara and Son. I will see you in the morning."

"Night, Dad."

"Goodnight, Joseph." Lara watched Joseph give a curt salute and walk into the house. She dropped her head, covering her eyes.

"What?"

"Aaaaah, I'm so embarrassed."

"Why, did I miss something?"

"Oh, my word, Josh, I nearly took my clothes off in front of your father."

"You did?" Josh said, looking surprised.

"I wanted to go for a swim and…" Lara's explanation was cut short as Josh erupted with laughter.

"What? It is not funny – what he must think of me?!"

"Sorry," Josh laughed again, "please don't worry, we skinny dip all the time."

"You do?"

"Yeah, my darling, but just not with our staff," he laughed again, "now drink your chocolate, Don Pedro," he said gently with his most sincere look.

Lara laughed. They both sat on one of the boulders surrounding the rock pool, dangling their feet in the water. They sipped their drinks and stared into the star-filled sky.

"It is beautiful here; your home is impressive."

"Well, it is my dad's. I have my own home in Knysna."

"Ah yes, I remember."

"Dad and I share; it does not make sense with me coming and going to have another home in Gauteng. Dad lives alone, and when I'm here, it is company for him in this huge place."

"Do you skinny dip?"

"All the time, it is very simple," Josh whispered. He stood up and, without a second thought, took off his clothes. He stood in front of Lara as naked as the day he was born. Lara's eyes grew wide. Her cheeks turned crimson. She blushed as he smiled at the fact that she had just given him the once-over. With that, Josh dived into the pool. Lara gasped, laughing at his white backside disappearing under the water. He surfaced with a grin on his face.

"Are you coming in?" He swam towards her, "Water's perfect," he squirted water at her through his teeth.

Lara was about to protest and then said, "Close your eyes!" Lara watched him squeeze his eyes shut, "No peeking!" In a flash, Lara undressed and quickly lowered herself into the water, ducking below the surface. She surfaced near to Josh, and before she could utter a word, Josh pulled her towards him and kissed her firmly on her mouth. Lara welcomed his soft lips and gentle embrace.

Lara felt his passion grow and groaned with delight as he kissed her neck and suckled on her lower lip. She bit gently on his chin and pushed her breasts into his chest. He cupped her breast, pressing her nipple gently between his thumb and forefinger. He groaned as she wrapped her legs around his waist. He kissed her again, this time with more passion. She showed her acceptance with a sensual whimper of her own.

CHAPTER 12

Blake ensured that his plan was irrevocably fine-tuned. He had run through it repeatedly until they all understood it perfectly. They drove quietly towards JDE. He was deep in thought. He was confident they were more than ready. He had not given a new life much thought, focusing instead on destroying the very men who had ultimately provided him the means to fulfil his desire for vengeance.

"We are here."

"Steady now, take a deep breath and smile," Blake said quietly and calmly.

They pulled up at the delivery entrance as the security guard put up his hand. He motioned for them to open the back of the Panel Van; Blake turned to Cliff, sitting in the back and nodded. Cliff opened the back door. The guard looked in and saw Cliff sitting among bouquets of flowers and cases of Champagne.

"We are here to set up the Champagne fountain for the party."

"Yeah, it looks like it," they both laughed.

The security guard checked his clipboard and waved them in. They parked and began to empty out the van. They carried everything to the service elevator, quickly packing it in. As the doors closed, they removed their overalls. They had the perfect penguin waiter outfits on underneath. They checked their guns and each other's appearance. They picked up the bouquets and cases of Champagne, standing poised for the doors to open.

Peter thrived on engaging people from different walks of life. This party was the essence of mixed cultures as their business dealt with a diverse group of developers and investors. Security was there to check their invites against the guest list. As always, Mrs Perkins was there to help him greet the guests as they arrived. He was grateful for the help. The caterers were busy with finishing touches, and he noted there were yet more bouquets arriving. He had not realised he had ordered so many flowers. He put it down to value for money.

"Well, Mrs Perkins, we have about fifteen minutes, and the floodgates will open."

"Not to worry, everything looks fabulous," she smiled at Peter, "you can be very proud of yourself."

"Could not have done it without you."

"I think you both have done a great job," Saul complimented them as he walked over to join them.

"Saul, hi," said Peter.

"This is Michelle," Saul introduced the lady on his arm.

"Lovely to meet you, Michelle. Please help yourself to a glass of bubbly," Peter offered.

"Thank you."

"Thanks, Peter," Saul said as he patted Peter on the shoulder.

Soon, the conference hall was filled with the who's who of the country's business leaders, celebrities, and socialites, all elegantly dressed and happily intermingling. The guest list was the envy of their competitors. Joseph arrived unaccompanied. He rarely brought a date to business functions, giving him the freedom to flirt with the beautiful women and discuss potential business opportunities as they arose.

"Peter! Josh arrived?" Joseph enquired.

"Not yet, Joseph."

"When he gets here, ask him to find me. We need to talk."

"Will do."

Lara had spent the best part of the day pampering herself. She had her hair and nails professionally done. To her surprise, Josh had sent her the most exquisite gown to wear. It arrived perfectly boxed with a ribbon and bow. Lara stood in the living room waiting for Josh to arrive. She was too nervous to sit in her dress, terrified she would wrinkle it. She walked over to the hall mirror and studied her appearance. Her makeup was subtle, and her eye shadow once again gave her eyes a smoky, sensual facade. Her hair was delicately pulled up, with curls falling loosely around her face. She looked sophisticated in her flesh-coloured, fitted evening gown. It showed off her figure beautifully, hugged her body and flared into a fishtail just above the knee. The gown's strapless bodice was covered in tiny Swarovski crystal beads. The crystals ran in abstract circular waves all the way down the gown. The fishtail flare was a combination of soft chiffon and stiff lace, which seemed to have a mind of its own. Lara was pleased. *I feel like a movie star,* she thought, smiling. With that, the doorbell rang. She felt a rush of adrenalin. *Josh!*

She opened the door, trying her best to do it casually.

"Wow, you look sensational."

"You don't look so shabby yourself," Lara gasped. She felt foolish, but Josh had literally taken her breath away. He was dressed in a midnight blue suit, a crisp white shirt, a self-tie bow tie, cufflinks, and elegant patent leather shoes. "Very handsome; the whole tuxedo look really suits you."

"Why thank you, my darling," Josh moved forward and kissed her tenderly.

"Hmm, I could do that all night," she whispered. "Josh, thank you so much for this exquisite dress. I love it."

"It was the greatest of pleasure," he whispered back. They kissed once more.

"We must get going. Traffic was a nightmare, and we are late."

"Lead the way, I'm ready." Lara closed the door behind them. They were both in high spirits, looking forward to the evening. Josh was keen to see Saul's face when he arrived with Lara on his arm. Peter had an inkling, and Joseph had witnessed more than they had wanted him to. Joseph asked them to play it low-key with regard to their relationship. They understood this was not the time and place. Lara had not even started working nor met all the staff yet. He was concerned about the optics.

Josh couldn't imagine life without Lara. Hiding his feelings was not an option. They had already been through so much for a new relationship, and it had only brought them closer. They arrived at JDE and were greeted by Mrs Perkins. If she was surprised that they were together, she never showed it. Peter grinned and greeted them with enthusiasm, and told Josh that his father was looking for him. Peter whispered something in Lara's ear, and she took his arm. They walked through the lively crowd and greeted guests. Josh entered the hall; he caught sight of Saul talking to his father. He stooped and scanned the room for Lara. He could not help himself. *Dad won't be pleased*, he thought, making his way over to her. As much as he tried to act casually around her, he was unable to resist running his hand across her back as he came to her side. He found her hand, and they intertwined their fingers. Saul took a double take when he saw Josh and Lara hand in hand. Josh laughed out loud.

"What's so funny?" Lara asked inquisitively.

"We have been noticed by the rest of the Board; Saul nearly swallowed his glass," Josh laughed again. Lara giggled as Josh led her through the people, pausing on occasion to greet a few guests.

"You look like a goddess; they can't take their eyes off you." Lara's eyes opened wide as she caught his. They both were smiling now. Happy. They were indeed the best-looking couple in the room. People were curious, but when they found out that she was a new consultant, it satisfied that curiosity. Eventually, they made their way towards his father and Saul.

"Josh, my Boy… Lara, you look beautiful."

"Thank you. Joseph, you look very handsome, too."

"Hello, Dad. Sorry we are late, but the traffic was horrendous with all the road works."

"Saul."

"Josh."

"Lara, nice to see you again," Saul said with a mischievous look in his eyes.

"You too, Saul. Peter has done a wonderful job putting this all together."

"Indeed, he really has the knack for this sort of thing," Saul turned to Michelle, "I'd like you to meet a friend of mine. This is Michelle," they all exchanged greetings, and Saul said, "Can I get you ladies something to drink?"

"I'd love some more Champers," Michelle said.

Lara smiled and said, "The same for me, thanks Saul."

Saul arrived with a tray of Champagne for everyone. Joseph and Josh were chatting away about the evening proceedings. Lara took a glass of Champagne from Saul and silently toasted Josh by lifting her glass in the air. Josh grinned and winked at her. Lara sipped her drink, feeling the bubbles tickle her nose. She could not take her eyes off Josh. She wondered if it was truly possible to feel this good. She attentively watched father and son deep in conversation. For the first time, she realised how alike Josh and Joseph were. She looked around the hall and was in awe of the suits and dresses. Beautiful flowers were everywhere. Candles gently flickering. Soft ballads playing in the background. *It's like something out of a fairy tale,* she thought to herself. Lara took a sip of her Champagne and looked up at Josh. He was staring at her... they smiled at each other. Suddenly, a deafening bang shot through the air! Time seemed to stop, and everything went motionless for a split second. Lara heard another thud, with an echo and saw blood burst from Joseph's chest as he was flung backwards. Before anyone could react, another loud bang rang out, and Saul's head seemed to explode with crimson Champagne. Lara felt Josh grab her waist and pull her to the floor. Lara landed hard with a thump, groaning in agony. He covered her body with his. She heard screaming, people running, falling over tables and chairs. More and more blasts... thud, thud, echoes, running into one another, *gunshots.* Before she knew what was happening, she heard Josh moan as his body went limp.

"Joshhh!" she screamed. Josh touched the back of his head; Lara could see he was hurt. She wasn't sure if he was shot or not. There was a man in a mask, gun in hand, standing over Josh; *he must have hit Josh from behind with the gun.* He kicked Josh in the stomach. She heard the air forced out of him. The man yanked Lara to her feet. Lara almost fell over; her dress was restricting. She looked around and saw people leaning over Joseph and Saul. She heard Josh calling to them. He looked up and saw the masked man holding Lara close to his body with his arm. Josh tried to get to his feet and stopped as he heard the click of the trigger being pulled back. He looked up and saw a gun pointed at Lara's head. He went ice cold.

"Don't do anything silly now; you don't want this pretty lady's blood on your hands. Stand up!"

Josh stood up slowly. He felt dizzy. Lara could see the fury in his eyes. He looked directly at her, and for a moment, his face softened. He rubbed the back of his neck, and his face grimaced as he looked at the two men lying motionless in their blood. He turned to the masked man.

"What do you want?"

"You."

"Well, you have me. Let her go."

"Move," he motioned Josh to the elevator. There was another burst of fire, and another masked individual shouted to everyone to lie face down on the floor. Lara and Josh were shoved into the elevator, and masks were put on their faces. The only difference was the masks they had on did not have holes for their eyes. Their wrists were duck-taped behind their backs. Masks lifted for a split, and their mouths were taped shut. They were walking blind.

Peter was the first to move once the elevator doors closed. He stood up and ran over to Saul and Joseph. He shuddered; Saul was dead. He moved to Joseph and felt for a pulse. He looked around and screamed, "Mrs Perkins, get an ambulance. Joseph, can you hear me," he ripped Joseph's shirt open and removed his tie, "Joseph, hold on, we are getting help." Joseph never made a sound. One of the guests came running up to Peter, "I'm a nurse, let me take a look at him," she checked his pulse, "It's weak, but there," she looked at his wound, "looks like it missed his heart, we need to put pressure on it, we need towels!"

Peter grabbed cloth serviettes off the tables, and they padded the wound. The nurse held pressure on the wound. People started to stand up. Women were crying. Michelle sat next to Saul, sobbing, rocking back and forth. The men began helping the women. Peter grabbed a tablecloth off the table and covered Saul's body, whispering under his breath, "Go with God, my friend."

Mrs Perkins came rushing up to Peter, "Ambulance is on its way. Security is checking the premises and contacted the Police. How is he?"

"Hanging in there."

"Saul?"

Peter shook his head and watched Mrs Perkins dissolve into tears, "What about Josh and Ms Sheffield?" she sobbed.

"Shit! Josh!" Peter leapt up and ran to the security. He found out that three caterers and a security guard had been shot and two guests fatally wounded. He filled them in on his take on the whole ordeal. Although everything had happened so fast. Josh and Lara were gone.

The Police arrived and started taking statements. Mrs Perkins did her best to provide coffee for those who wanted and brandy for most who were in shock. They took Joseph off in the ambulance to a private clinic in Rosebank. Peter wanted desperately to go with Joseph, but he knew that Joseph was well cared for, and he needed to concentrate on Josh and Lara. He also needed to ensure that JDE was in good hands.

Peter spoke to the staff to comfort them and requested they all lend a hand in making sure JDE got back on its feet come Monday morning. Peter was the next in line what with Joseph, Josh, and Saul out of the picture. Peter's heart sank at the thought, but he was confident with what organisational skills he had. He could hold this all together. It was not the way he wanted a promotion, albeit a temporary one.

It was well into the early hours of the morning when all the statements were taken and guests were allowed to leave. Peter sat at the bar sipping whisky on the rocks. His hands trembled. It occurred to him the music was still going, and *Cats in The Cradle* was playing. His heart sank.

"You need to get some sleep, Peter," Mrs Perkins stood next to him with her hand on his shoulder."

"Mrs Perkins, thank you for all your help tonight, but you should go home."

"I'm on my way… I just wanted to let you know that Joseph is in surgery."

"Thank you. I'm going there now."

"Would you like me to go with you?"

"No, you go and get some sleep." He stood up and gave her a hug. "Will you be okay?"

"Yes, thanks, I am going with Michelle. She needs a ride home. I will go to the hospital tomorrow; I will go past Mr Dillon's house and get a few things for him."

"Thanks, that would be appreciated."

"Night."

"Night," Mrs Perkins kissed Peter on the cheek and walked away.

Peter had never known her to be affectionate and was certain he had never seen her cry. It brought tears to his eyes, and then, as the evening events ran through his head, Peter Patterson wept uncontrollably.

CHAPTER 13

Peter stirred from an uncomfortable sleep as a trolly rolled noisily by. He rubbed his eyes and looked at his watch. He went over to the nurse's desk.

"Joseph Dillion; is he out of surgery?" he asked, surprised at how drained and croaky he sounded. He watched the nurse scan her computer.

"Yes, just out of recovery. They are moving him to the ICU on the third floor," she said, pointing to the elevators. Peter nodded with thanks and walked over to the elevators.

Josh woke up with a jolt. He could smell coffee. Lara stirred in his arms and began to wake up with the realisation that it was not a dream but a very real nightmare.

"Good. You are both awake," Blake said, standing at a table holding three mugs.

Josh blinked to clear his vision, staring at the figure in front of him. *It couldn't be, could it? He looks so different, hardly recognisable,* he thought.

"Blake?" he asked disbelievingly. "What the...?"

"Hello, nephew. Apologies for the boys. They are a little less forgiving than I am," he said, placing the mugs on the table. "I'm not an animal, Josh, so let's have a cup of coffee and a civil conversation," he said, picking up a knife and walking towards them. He helped Lara to her feet, sat her down on a bale of hay and handed her two mugs of coffee. He motioned towards Josh to join her. *Clever!* Josh thought. *Not to get too close to me.* Lara handed him a mug, their eyes met, and for a second, it was about a cup of coffee and nothing more.

"Mr Patterson?"

"Yes," Peter said, turning while holding the elevator doors open.

"Detective Sergeant Ed Matsinye, we spoke at JD Enterprises yesterday,"

"Yes, of course," Peter said, shaking his hand. "Any news on Josh and Lara?"

"Are you going up to see Mr Dillion?"

"I was hoping to, but I'm not sure if he will be awake or even if they will let me into ICU."

"Let's talk on the way up, and maybe I can help with that," the detective said as he stepped into the elevator and pushed the third-floor button.

"I can't believe this is happening," Peter said, rubbing his hands through his hair. "Do you have any idea where they are?" Peter started to sound hysterical.

"We are certain that Blake Henry is behind the abduction; security footage led us to that conclusion. Although, they had camera interference which distorted the footage," Detective Matsinye explained, almost looking convinced with what he was saying. Peter had no words; he just shook his head, regretting not taking Blake's threat more seriously.

Ed recognised that look of despair and said, "We are hoping Mr Dillion Snr will have some insight as to where he may be."

They walked onto the ICU floor only to be met by interleading glass doors that read 'Staff Only'.

"Ring that bell," Ed said, gesturing his head toward the button while using the disinfectant on his hands. Peter pushed the bell and disinfected his hands. It wasn't long before a Nursing Sister appeared at the door and told them that Joseph was still sedated and would not be up to visitors for at least 24 hours. Ed left his card and said, "His son may not have 24 hours. Please call me as soon as he wakes up." The Nurse looked surprised and quickly nodded, taking a look at the card. They had hardly left the hospital when the Sister called and said Joseph was awake and anxious to see them. They looked at each other and rushed back inside.

"Blake, the coffee is appreciated, but what the hell are you thinking?" Josh said, sipping the steaming black liquid.

"I am here because of *you,* Josh, golden boy. I'm going to get what is due to me and then some. Then, if your father makes it, he witnesses the fall of JD Enterprises.

"What do you mean if my father makes it?" The colour drained from his face as he remembered his father had been flung back the night before.

Lara grimaced as she touched her lips and cut on her cheek. She looked at Josh with concern showing on her face. Blake got up and handed her a cloth and a bottle of water, "Here, clean yourself up."

"Thank you," Lara said quietly.

"Blake, my father – what do you know?"

"Not much. He is alive for now, but we don't have time for this," the tone of his voice changed as he opened his laptop. "You, my young man, just need to sign into JDE's bank account and transfer every cent into the provided beneficiary accounts. It's as simple as that." He looked up at Josh and smiled, showing his oddly coated gold teeth. *Josh wondered what that was all about.*

"I get it, this is all about money, but I don't have those details, Blake. You are the finance guru, so you should know that." Josh put his mug down and stood up, moving towards Blake. He stopped in his tracks as Seth stepped out of the dark, holding a revolver. Josh put up his hands, "No need for that."

Blake motioned to Seth to step back.

"Josh, you seem to think this is a negotiation. It is not. If you don't do it, I will have Seth put a bullet in your girlfriend's head," Blake threatened as he stood up, using the knife to point to the chair. Josh walked over and sat in front of the computer. Blake had really done his homework and set it all up to transfer. Josh looked over at Lara.

"Lara has nothing to do with this, Blake. I want your word you will let her go?"

"You have my word. I will let you both go; I am not a monster." Josh took a deep breath and began to type; Blake was about to check when Seth pointed the revolver and shot Blake in the head. Lara screamed, and Josh jumped back, staring at Blake lying in the dirt. Seth put the revolver to Josh's head.

Joseph looked deathly pale. Peter refrained from reacting. They both greeted Joseph and lied about how good he looked after having just been shot.

"Thanks. Peter, you look like shite!" Joseph whispered, trying not to laugh. "Is Josh here?" It was Peter who now looked pale. He couldn't bring himself to speak and glanced at Ed for assistance. Realising the old man was unaware that Josh and Lara were abducted, Ed responded, "Mr Dillion, I am sorry to inform you, but both your son and Ms Sheffield were taken during the attack on JD Enterprises."

"What? I don't understand, taken, what does that mean?"

"Kidnapped," Peter murmured as he watched Joseph's eyes widen.

"Actually," Ed said, stepping forward, holding his hand up, worried Joseph would pop a stitch or worse, have a heart attack, "we don't know if it was a kidnapping as there has been no call for ransom as far as we can ascertain." Joseph tried to sit up... they both rushed to his aid.

"Where's my phone," he was unnervingly calm in his request, but the urgency did not go unnoticed. Peter looked in the drawer next to the hospital bed and found his phone.

"Good idea, they may have called you," Peter exclaimed, watching Joseph check his phone.

"No, I can do one better!" Joseph turned his phone around and showed the detective the screen. On the screen, there was a map and a little red dot blinking.

"Fuck yeah!" Ed shouted. He took out his own mobile and called the Police station, "Mike, we found Dillion and Sheffield. I am sending you the coordinates. Get the Special Task Force there immediately." He hung up. There was no need for formalities. Mike knew the drill. "Mr Dillion, Peter, thank you; time is of the essence. I will call you later," he said, leaving with the Police radio in hand.

Joseph looked at Peter and let out a gasp as Ed disappeared through the door. All they heard was, "All units, this is Detective Matsinye Code 3. I repeat Code 3 - two 920A's, proceed with caution. Go, go, go!"

With the revolver pointed at Josh's head, Seth insisted, "Sit! A change of bank details," he said, handing Josh a piece of paper. With that, Cliff came strolling into the shed.

"Is it done?" Seth said to Cliff.

Cliff threw the shovel down, "Yes, all done."

Lara looked at Josh. The situation had just escalated dangerously. "Guys! Let's take a minute here," Josh said, trying to calm the situation. "I am happy to do the transfer, but have you thought this through... how will you get away with this? Do you have a plan?"

"Sit and do the transfer," Seth shouted and turned to Cliff, "Watch her." Josh sat and began to type once again. He noticed that Blake's knife was lying at his foot; he looked at Lara and looked down and saw that she had seen it.

"Sorry, I made a mistake," Josh said softly, and Seth leaned in. With that, Josh kicked the knife over to Lara and lifted the laptop, smashing it into Seth's face. The gun went flying, and Josh dived for it. Lara grabbed the knife and lunged towards Cliff. They both fell, and Cliff landed on top of her. Josh's focus shifted, worried about Lara. At that moment, Seth got the upper hand and pointed the gun at Josh. There was a loud crack in the air. Josh shut his eyes and waited for the pain. It didn't come. He looked over to Seth and watched him fall forward, with Ed Matsinye standing behind him, holding a gun. An army of riot Police rushed in. Josh quickly moved over to Cliff, lying on top of Lara. She was moaning, "I can't breathe," she whispered.

"Lara! Are you okay?!" he shouted, pushing Cliff off her. "You're bleeding!"

"No, it is not mine," she said, touching her bloodied gown. The blood was Cliff's, who had run into the knife, falling onto Lara. He bled out quickly.

"Josh, Lara?! Are you both okay?" Ed shouted as he ran over to them.

"Yes, thanks; we are now," Josh said with relief in his voice.

"Blake?"

"Over there," Josh pointed. "He didn't make it."

"Did you do that?"

Josh shook his head, "Not me. That was greed."

"Josh... the transfer?" Lara murmured the words.

"I never did it," he said, pulling her close and kissing her on her forehead. He looked at the detective and asked, "How did you find us?"

"You have your father to thank."

"Is he alright?"

"Yes, he will need a lot of rest, but I believe he'll make a full recovery."

"Thank the Lord," Josh prayed before asking, "What did you mean when you said we have my dad to thank?"

"It turns out he put a tracker in your signate ring," Ed said, raising his eyebrows and smiling. Josh looked at his hand at his gold 21st birthday gift and laughed. *Go, Dad!*

Joseph lay looking out the hospital window. Although the view was obscured by more hospital windows, he got a glimpse of the fiery sky. *What a wonderful sunset it would be at Chantilly.* His thoughts were of family and how close he had come to losing his son. That was a terrifying thought. He had loved and lost his soul mate. Another life and death-event was something he could not contemplate again. He was sure he would never survive it. Josh had called to say he and Lara were alright, just distraught about what they had been through. *Rightfully so,* he thought.

"Dad!" Josh walked into the ward.

"Josh? Boy, am I glad to see you. Are you okay? How is Lara?"

"We are fine, Dad. Please don't tire yourself with all this. How are you feeling?"

"I was shot. How do you think I am feeling?" he said, trying not to laugh, wincing in pain.

"I was kidnapped, and I am not complaining!" They both laughed.

"Did anyone call Grace?

"Yes, I filled her in. She wanted to fly up. I managed to talk her off that ledge."

"Yeah, not necessary. Sweet of her, but not necessary. Did you hear the news about Saul?

"Yeah. It is unbelievable, Dad. I'm so sorry for your loss." Josh knew his dad would take this hard. Saul was his best friend, golfing buddy and all-round 'champ'. "I spoke to Peter earlier. It's tragic. I will miss him terribly, and so will JDE." Josh said. *We have some hard work to do to sort this all out, both in the business and personally,* he thought. Josh filled his father in with the events that took place and how Blake's cronies had turned on him. *Poetic justice.* As light-hearted as one was about it, it was a bitter pill to swallow. Josh cringed at the thought of what Lara had been through and what could have happened. They turned their discussion to the next steps regarding JD Enterprises. They agreed an informal conference would help the process. Josh confirmed that they would fly the management team to Chantilly for a long weekend, for a bit of R&R, and to regroup. They agreed they would leave after Saul's memorial. Josh could see his father was battling to keep his eyes open, and the nurses were hovering. He kissed his dad on his forehead and left.

Josh made a few calls as he left the hospital. He called Mrs Perkins and asked her to notify Peter, Simon and Lara of plans and to draw up an itinerary. Josh was saddened at the realisation that Saul would not be there. He felt himself shaking his head, still in disbelief at what was an awful fact. *They were now two people short around the Boardroom table, a gentleman like Saul and the traitor Blake turned out to be*, he thought. He let Steve know that the jet should be ready for a full passenger list, destination George Airport, and then a transfer to Knysna for a long weekend.

Joseph spent a few more days in hospital, and Josh took care of several business issues brought about by the whole saga. He was happy to fly with the other guests. He called Grace to check on Wrinkles and to warn her that they would be a full house from Thursday to Sunday in two weeks' time. He was confident Grace would have it all in hand. She always said, "Never fear, young man, I have caterers and housekeepers on speed dial should we need them."

He also phoned Lara, who was desperate to see her family and loved the idea – especially under these circumstances. *At least I can offer a little comfort.* He warned her that she would also get a formal JDE invite via Mrs Perkins as there would be a work discussion over the weekend.

Lara stepped out of a hot shower. Her skin was inflamed after the way she had scrubbed herself. She shuddered at the thought of those animals touching her. Blake was a bastard for what he did, and she couldn't help thanking God he had put an end to what could have been a life-changing event. Lara sat at her dressing table and cleaned her face, applied moisturiser, and then lashings of hand and body lotion to her arms, elbows, and hands – a routine that was as normal for her and its comforting familiarity was something she very much needed.

For a second, she found her own eyes staring back at her in the mirror and then realised her teeth were clenched and she was frowning. She stopped and looked into her troubled eyes and broke down in tears. She was not sure for how long she cried. She still managed to open a bottle of 'vino', sobbing through the entire bottle and dancing around her bed to Billy Joel's 'Second Wind'.

Emotionally drained, she lay on her bed. She stared at the ceiling, wishing she had filled the water bottle next to her bed. *This too shall pass*, she thought as images of Josh filled her head before she drifted off to sleep.

CHAPTER 14

Steve was busy checking the flight plan. Nine souls onboard, including crew. Destination George Airport, Western Cape. He had done a head count and was amazed at how well Joseph was looking, having just taken a bullet to the chest. Josh and Lara had arrived with him. Simon and Mrs Perkins were already onboard, waiting. Julian, Peter's assistant, was last to arrive.

The two-hour flight was pleasant and over in what felt like no time at all. Josh had organised a shuttle to transport them to Chantilly. He and Lara took his Jeep as it was still at the airport. Josh and Lara were determined to make this weekend pleasant and fruitful. They agreed to make it a healing journey for all. Lara had called Stacey and invited them over for dinner that evening.

They arrived at Chantilly with Wrinkles bounding over to the car, practically jumping into Josh's arms. Lara grinned, not sure who was more delighted to see the other as both were squealing.

Grace stood at the door with a smile on her face and ushered everyone into the house, pointing out where the guest rooms were. Lara giggled as Josh was very quick to usher her to his suite. Tranquillity filled the house, and Grace rallied around Joseph like a mother hen. She had also arranged scrumptious lunch platters and Champagne in all the rooms. It was a welcome respite to take a breather, unpack and just chill for the afternoon.

Late afternoon, everyone started to filter onto the patio. Josh played barmen while Peter lit the firepit. Grace provided endless eats for all.

The sun was setting over the water. The doorbell rang. "Aah, the doorbell," Josh said, pushing the Champagne back into the ice bucket. "I'll get it; it must be Rob and Stacey."

"I'll come with you," Lara said.

He opened the door. "Rob," he shook his hand, "Stacey, welcome."

"What a beautiful home, Josh... hello sister," Stacey and Lara hugged, doing a little jig.

"Josh, thanks for the nod," said Rob. "Hey Lara, how are you doing kiddo?" The tenderness in his voice did not go unnoticed. Lara hugged Rob, and they all walked in, chatting about Chantilly.

Josh made the necessary introductions, poured more drinks, and everyone settled in comfortably. The conversation was kept as light as the moon that shone brightly over the water. Grace rang a gong for dinner. *So posh,* Lara thought, but loving it all the same. Josh quickly explained it was an ancient relic his grandfather had found in Indonesia. "Grace loves to feed people and calls it her Num-Num drum." Everyone shrieked with laughter. The sound echoed over the lake and into the still night.

Joseph stood at the head of the table, tapping his crystal goblet, "A toast to Grace for this wonderful spread, to the wonderful company tonight, and to absent family and friends. Cheers!"

"Cheers," they all raised their glasses in unison.

"Josh, I hear the fishing is great in these parts," Julian said with excitement.

"I've been known to catch a fish or two."

"Actually," Grace jumped in and said, "we are enjoying Josh's latest catch as we speak."

"This is incredible. Thank you, Josh and Grace," Mrs Perkins said.

"Hopefully, we can get some fishing in this weekend," Peter added.

"If you guys are up to it, Mullet fishing could be on the cards tonight."

"I'm not a fisherman but would love to give it a go," Simon said awkwardly.

"No worries, Simon. You're with a couple of local lads. We've got your back," Rob said, laughing and raising his glass. Lara shook her head. There was more squealing at the table. *Men! They are so easy to please,* she mused.

The conversation pretty much stayed on Mullet fishing, who would hold the torch and who would scoop the net. Simon was thrilled to hear that fishing rods were not the order of the evening.

Dinner was over, and everyone moved back to the firepit.

"So where is the boat moored?" Simon asked eagerly.

Josh laughed, "You see that wooden boat lying on the bank near the jetty?"

"Yeah."

"Well, that is G&T. Finest rowing boat on the lake... and my baby."

"Can we all fit?" There was a roar of laughter from the patio.

"No, but we will get Bye-Bye Birdy out. She is in the shed. Dad's pride and joy."

"I can't go with my shoulder. I will keep the ladies' company," Joseph muttered.

"You guys take the gear to G&T. I will fetch Bye-Bye Birdy."

"I'll give you a hand, Simon offered.

They collected the nets, torches, and cooler bags. "Guys, wait for us. We can launch together," Josh called out.

Joseph watched as they all set off in different directions. Joseph smiled and shook his head, reminded of a time when he had watched the kids doing the exact same thing years before many times.

"Well, ladies, I know where the marshmallows are kept."

"Can I get them for you?" Lara said.

Joseph smiled, lifted the lid of his side table and presented marshmallows, chocolate, biscuits, and twin forks to take two at a time. He grinned from ear to ear. "Ladies, shall we?"

Mrs Perkins and Grace joined Joseph while Lara and Stacey stood on the balcony watching the men walk down to the jetty. With that, Simon and Josh came walking past with a smaller upside-down version of G&T over their heads. Josh lifted the boat above his head and winked at Lara as they went past.

Julian and Peter reached G&T. Rob turned to see Josh and Simon battling with the oars as well as the boat, "Guys, I'm going to give Josh a hand," he said, shouting back towards Josh and Simon.

"No worries, we got this. Grab that side, Julian," Peter said, pointing to the bow of G&T.

Lara and Stacey were remarking about how beautiful the reflection of the moon looked on the water and what an incredible spot Chantilly was. Then boom!!! A loud bang tore through the air, followed by a deafening roar and a crisp white flash. The jetty turned into a fireball hurtling up and out. Rob was thrown forward into the air toward the house and then dropped like a stone. The explosion sent a shock wave that knocked Simon and Josh off their feet back towards the shed. Hot air filtered the screams; burning shards of wood flew in all directions as sheets of water rose in the air for what seemed like an eternity. Everything stopped. And then mayhem broke out. There was a thud, thud, thud as splinters and falling leaves rained down, followed by a crash of water on water. A tree had caught fire, and there was smoke billowing into the sky.

"Jean!" Joseph screamed! He had not used her name in years. Mrs Perkin grabbed her phone and started dialling. "Grace! First aid kits now!"

Joseph grimaced as he tried to move, still holding onto a burning marshmallow. "Lara, Stacey, are you okay? Can you get down there?" Both women were in shock but were nodding and shaking at the same time.

"Lara, move!" Stacey shouted, taking her by the hand as they both scrambled down the stairs, stumbling over debris. "You check on them," Stacey pointed in the direction of Josh and Simon. Stacey continued running towards the jetty and almost fell over Rob. "No, no, Rob! Rob, can you hear me?" He was lying face down in the dirt. She did not want to turn him over. Confused, he managed to move himself. As he did, Stacey saw he was bleeding profusely from his head. She took her jacket off and held it to the back of his head. "Don't move, honey. Help is on its way," she said, looking around.

The smoke was lifting. Grace was making her way to Stacey with a first aid kit. Stacey looked over to Bye Bye Birdy. Josh and Simon were still under the boat, on the ground, and seemed somehow to be lodged deeper in the boat. Only their torsos and legs were visible. She turned to look at the jetty and saw Peter and Julian a few feet away from the blast zone. *What the fuck happened!* She thought, confused. She turned back to Rob. "Honey? Rob, can you hear me?" Rob groaned.

"Here you go, Stacey," Grace said, unzipping the first aid pack. They dug for bandages, then did the best they could to bandage Rob's bleeding head. Stacey looked around again and saw Mrs Perkins helping Lara and could hear Joseph talking on the phone. She looked at Grace and asked, "Could you stay with Rob? I need to check on Peter and Julian." Grace, looking pale, nodded.

Lara ran as fast as she could towards the boat. She could not see much because of the smoke except for two motionless bodies sticking out from under the boat. *Josh, please be okay.* She wasn't aware she was yelling their names or if it was Joseph shouting out Josh's name. Wrinkles was barking and sniffing around Josh while digging furiously in the dirt. As Lara got to the boat, she dropped to the ground and tried everything she could to move the boat off the men. Mrs Perkins arrived at her side, and together, they pushed the boat over. Both men were unconscious. Lara felt for a pulse; they were alive. Almost simultaneously, they woke up, coughing and disorientated.

"Easy does it. Are you okay? Anything hurt?" Lara asked Josh gently.

"What the – what happened?!" Josh was shouting. "My ears are ringing!"

"Ahhh, my head," Simon said, wincing.

"Josh! Lara, are they okay?" Joseph was hanging over the balcony. He saw Josh put his thumb up and was relieved, "Help is on its way."

"Lara, I can't breathe."

"What can I do?"

"Stop squeezing me so tight."

"Oh, sorry, sorry," she said as she loosened the tightness of her embrace.

They all looked up when they heard Stacey screaming for help.

"Go, help, we are right behind you!" Josh said, ushering Lara on. He got up and helped Simon to his feet.

"What the fuck happened, Josh? Did the boat engine explode?"

"Definitely not. Rowing boats don't have engines."

"Simon, run and get fire extinguishers from the house's front door and kitchen. Bring them down to the jetty."

"Will do. Shit, I hope they are okay."

"You and me both."

Josh checked on Rob, who was sitting up, holding his head. By the time he got to the lake, it was apparent that Julian was dead, recognisable only by his blue sweatshirt. Lara had covered his head with her jacket. He turned to see Lara and Stacey kneeling over Peter; he was barely breathing, and they were applying pressure on most of his body. Mrs Perkins was handing them gauze and bandages. The symphony of sirens filled the night air, then flashing red lights, followed by flashing blue lights with the assurance that help had arrived and a promise that Peter may just make it.

The ambulance roared off down the long driveway. The Fire Department put the fires out while the Police demarcated the crime scene. Peter and Rob were on their way to the hospital. Stacey and Lara followed in Rob's Ranger. Simon and Josh were treated on-site for minor cuts and bruises. They were counting their blessings. Grace and Mrs Perkins were making coffee and sandwiches for the Fire Department crew. Josh and Joseph sat by the firepit, staring into the flames, sipping very expensive single malt scotch.

"We are drinking the good stuff, I see," Josh commented as he sipped.

"Son, at this rate, we are not going to live long enough to drink it, so now is as good a time as any."

"You're not kidding," Josh said, looking towards what was left of the jetty. Wrinkles curled up at his feet. "Did they find anything?"

"Don't know, the Forensic guys are gathering samples for analysis of post-explosion residues. They did mention a type of Improvised Explosive Device (IED), perhaps set under G&T. It would have exploded at the slightest touch."

"I am the only one who uses her, so it makes sense that the bomb was meant for me." Josh looked down, his brow furrowed, looking drained. "I got Julian killed... and maybe Peter."

"Not a thought I even want to contemplate, Son, and this is not on you."

"What about the rest of the house?"

"Cameras were checked. The jetty is the only blind spot, but they swept the house and are satisfied that was the only IED."

The rest of the evening turned into a national inquisition. Statements taken from Josh, Joseph, Simon, Grace, and Mrs Perkins. The Police had said they would go via the hospital to take the rest of the statements. Lara had gone home with Stacey. They reported that Rob was staying in the hospital overnight for observations. Peter was in the ICU after his surgery. The ladies retired exhausted.

"Can I join you?" Simon said, walking onto the patio, looking refreshed from his shower.

"Of course, grab a glass… we have the good stuff."

"Thanks, any news?" Simon said, handing a glass to Josh.

"Nothing new; we know what and how, but why is the question,"

"Blake. It has to be him. It had to be part of his overall plan from the start," Joseph said, clenching his teeth.

"That would make sense. During our investigation, I read Blake's profile, and he was in South African Special Forces."

"Recces, yes, I remember that, so he had explosives training for sure," Joseph said, nodding his head. Simon nodded in agreement.

They chatted well into the night over the bottle of whisky, debating the idea that Blake was behind the bomb. They agreed Blake had the knowledge, the means, and the motive. The general feeling was that he had set this all up prior to the kidnapping, knowing that Josh would eventually check on the boat or go fishing. The blast was clearly designed to kill Josh and hurt Joseph if he survived the first attack. It was hard to think that was the only booby trap, but the Police dogs had not found any other devices. Were they in the clear? No one really knew for sure.

Simon eventually announced he did not enjoy mullet fishing and was going to bed. They watched him sway through the door. The width of the doorway seemed to be the issue. Joseph called it a night. Josh, feeling inebriated, stumbled a bit, helping his father to his room. He wished his dad a good night and continued to his suite. He grimaced, feeling his cuts and bruises as he strolled down the passage. He opened the door and leaned against the doorframe to steady himself. He was pleasantly surprised to find Lara peacefully asleep, her face and body bathed in the soft light of the waning moon.

CHAPTER 15

Lara stirred from a restless sleep with Josh making love to her. It was wonderful. It was sensual. He made it so. Josh was that kind of man, gentle and generous. The act of lovemaking was just that, the making of an intense love. Two bodies in motion growing more intense with each surge. Lovelier each time. Close-fitting. Their reality was boundless. A simultaneous shudder. Exquisite truth revealed.

"Thank you for coming back," he whispered while kissing her neck.

"Hmmm. Grace, let me in,"

"Yeah?" he murmured, continuing his gentle kisses over her shoulder.

"I needed a moment to myself… soaked in a hot bath. You guys looked like you were doing what was needed."

"Guess so? There was a lot to unpack."

"Was that a case of whisky?" they both laughed as Josh sat up and thumped her softly with a pillow.

They chatted until the sun came up. There was so much they needed to say to each other. They had found each other in the grip of traumatic events.

"Is that coffee I smell?" Lara asked.

"Would you like some?"

"You have a coffee machine in your room," Lara said, eyebrows raised as she questioned him.

"Well, it is more of a morning alarm, but yes, my dad and I both have wet bars in our suites," he said, winking at her. "Besides, I know how to show a lady a good time, one cup at a time."

"I wouldn't go that far. Since we met, I have been shot at, kidnapped, assaulted, almost blown up," she was interrupted as Josh kissed her deeply.

"Hush, my lovely coffee is ready," Josh jumped up, and Lara giggled with delight as she watched his bare bottom disappear into the bathroom. *Oh lordy*, she thought, pulling the duvet over her head to mask her laughing. *The man is hot!*

Josh came out of the bathroom dressed in a luxurious white bathrobe. He handed her one and said, "Put this on. Meet me on the deck. I'll bring the coffee."

Josh and Lara lounged on the deck under a warm blanket. They watched the sun come up and drank the strong black coffee from hand-pottered mugs. The sunrise was stunning, with pink and purple hues blanketing the water as they looked on. Knysna was like that. There was always something different to see and do. New. Fresh. From sunrises to sunsets, pottery cups or a seventy-two-meter abseil from The Heads. They chatted about the new and improved jetty that would replace the pile of charred wood lying in the water, enjoying the warmth of their togetherness.

Soon, the house was buzzing with Police and nosy neighbours. Grace naturally served up a buffet breakfast feast for all. Josh had called Ed Matsinye and filled him in on their Blake theory. Ed agreed it was an interesting theory, but he was concerned that some things just were not adding up. He was not ready to go into detail and promised to call with an update. A deep, resounding voice called, "Josh?!"

"In here, Dad," Josh replied, "shouldn't you be resting?"

"I'll rest when I am dead. I just spoke to the hospital, and Peter is stable."

"That is fantastic news!"

"The Police have more questions; they are in your office."

"Simon?"

"He is with them."

"Good, hopefully, they have answers for us. Then we need to sit down and make some decisions about the company."

"Isn't that the truth," Josh added, following his father into his office.

The Police confirmed that it was an Improvised Explosive Device (IED) planted under the boat that had caused the devastating explosion. Although it was powerful, it was not made by a professional. Shockingly, a bird, squirrel, or harsh weather elements could have detonated the device. They said there would be a full forensic investigation into the matter. A clearer picture would hopefully emerge. *Josh shuddered at the thought of Wrinkles playing down there.* The report was of little comfort. There were more questions than answers. *Who put it there? When did they put it there? If it was so sensitive, it had to be recent?*

The Police left, and Joseph called an impromptu meeting to chat about the immediate issue they had with JD Enterprises. The meeting went on for most of the morning. It was evident that everyone was exhausted, and Joseph left them with a few ideas to consider and insisted they get some rest. They would discuss it over dinner that evening.

Ed Matsinye had received a copy of the Forensics Report from the Knysna SAPS office. He was troubled. The timeline did not make sense. If the Forensic Report was to be believed, Blake Henry was murdered before the IED was placed. This was an amateur-made device at best, although lethal and detonated by a mobile phone. Ed grabbed his jacket and headed out the door. He made a few calls. An hour later, Steve, JDE's pilot, was waiting for him on the airstrip.

Josh and Joseph were the first to arrive on the deck. The firepit was crackling away, sending sparks into the air. Josh went behind the bar and poured two whiskeys on the rocks. He handed one to his father, "You ready for this?"

"We are about to find out."

Mrs Perkins and Grace appeared with platters of Canapés served in teardrop porcelain spoons. Josh poured a glass of Champagne for each of them. Lara and Simon entered together. Lara had been to check on Rob and Stacey. Simon helped Josh with the drinks. The conversation quickly turned to JDE. They all chatted about who could possibly take on Saul's position as head of the Architectural Department. They agreed it was time to promote long-time employee Amanda Henning. She was a top-class graduate from the University of Witwatersrand's School of Architecture and Planning. It was a unanimous choice. Blake's position was trickier as they needed an experienced CFO. Simon had offered to throw his hat into the ring as he was a qualified Chartered Accountant with an MBA. Joseph was happy to add him to the shortlist. Joseph then asked Lara if she would be interested in the position of acting Marketing Director until Peter was well enough to return to work. She was thrilled to help as it would be easier to complete her rebranding project from within the company. Decisions were made. There was a clink of glasses. Grace lifted the Webber lid and removed the pork and apple belly roast. Everyone headed to the dining room for another one of Grace's feasts. Grace hit the gong.

After dinner, everyone was relaxed. Joseph had made his famous Irish coffees, and Grace served her dark chocolate truffle balls. Josh slipped away from the dinner table, and when he returned, Ed Matsinye was with him.

"You all have met Detective Ed Matsinye?" he said.

"Evening all, apologies for the interruption," the Detective offered.

"Not at all. Come…" Joseph gestured to the lounge, "Let's all retire to the lounge, and the good Detective can update us with the latest news on the case." Everyone walked towards the lounge with a drink and truffle in hand. They all laughed; no one was leaving their truffle! Grace blushed but secretly was pleased they all had a good time.

"Ed, can we offer you a drink?" Josh said as he showed him into the lounge.

"Just coffee, please – black, no sugar."

Lara caught Mrs Perkins' eye; both had the same thought: *He was clearly here on business*. Grace got up to fetch coffee for the Detective. The others made themselves comfortable, chuckling and whispering to each other. At this point, the atmosphere was still upbeat, a little excited even at the prospect of an update of all the events that had taken place.

Joseph, Josh, Lara, Simon, Mrs Perkins, and Grace sat poised, waiting for the Detective to speak. To their surprise, Steve, Rob and Stacey walked in.

"Hi everyone," Stacey said. Rob and Steve followed suit with a hand wave.

"Hey, Sis, Rob," Lara uttered, confused that they arrived at this late hour. The pilot was a confusing addition. *Maybe he stayed over before flying back.* The thought ran through her head.

"Welcome. Come in, please. Can we get you something to drink?" Josh said, heading for the bar.

"Please," Rob said with Steve in tow.

"Anyone else?" There was a shared murmur of "*please*" from the room. The mood was not as cheerful as before. Ed patiently drank his coffee and ate the truffle that was offered to him. Lara caught a glimpse of police officers walking around the house. She quickly looked at Josh, and he just winked at her. *So, he knew what this was all about.* She sipped her wine. She leant over to Stacey and mumbled, "Col. Mustard did it in the billiard room with the candle stick."

"You nailed it," Stacey whispered, "but the question is, who the fuck is Col. Mustard." she continued, raising her eyebrows. They both laughed nervously.

Ed stood up, took his glasses off and cleaned them. As if he was trying to gather his thoughts. "This investigation is ongoing; however, we still have questions," he checked his glasses and put them back on. "Unfortunately, this is time-sensitive. Bear with us. You will be individually taken through your statement from yesterday." There was little reaction from everyone until he added, "Please don't leave this room unless you are called upon, and if you wouldn't mind, put your mobile phones in the basket." They exchanged glances and quickly stood up and handed their phones to the uniformed Policeman holding the basket.

"I'll go first," Josh offered. Ed nodded, and they both left the room.

"Where do you want to set up?" Josh asked the Detective.

"Somewhere with one entrance, not too comfortable."

"Wine cellar?"

"That could work," Ed said. "Lead the way."

Josh ushered Ed down a wide stone staircase to a double glass door. Two tall, standing cast iron candelabras proudly guarded the entrance. Josh hit a switch, and the candles ignited. Ed smiled suitably impressed. Inside the cellar, an antique wrought iron chandelier hung in the centre, impressively dangling over an oak wood table with wrought iron table legs and four matching chairs. The wine cellar was walled out in stone, with several well-stocked wine racks running the length of the room. A coffee machine in the corner flanked with a few mugs sat perfectly on a wine barrel next to a fridge with chilled stock and bottles of water. Ed was suitably fascinated. They chatted about the theory Ed had. Josh made coffee while Ed moved two chairs from the table.

Ed sat across the table from Josh. He pulled out a file and a recording device. He held up a finger, motioning to Josh to be silent, and pushed play. Ed gave his full name, time, and date. He introduced Joshua Dillion and had him verbally acknowledge his identity and that he agreed that the interview would be recorded. "Josh, in your own words, state your recollection of events from the time you landed in George."

"We landed around 15h00 at George Airport, and we had arranged transport to accommodate all our guests. Including myself, there were eight of us: my father, Joseph Dillion, Lara Sheffield, Simon Fielding, Jean Perkins, Peter Patterson, and Julian Lang. My Jeep was at the airport. Lara and I drove here together. Steve Harding, our company pilot, went his own way. He would stay in the area to fly us back on Monday morning first thing. We arrived at Chantilly, my home, roughly 45 minutes later. Grace McDonald, our housekeeper, greeted us, and we all found our rooms. Everyone did their own thing; Lara and I chatted and had a late lunch in my suite."

"Did you see anyone else or talk to anyone else?"

"Not that I recall. Lara was on the balcony. She was on her mobile phone talking to her sister."

"Do you know why?" Ed asked.

"Catching up and inviting her sister and her husband to dinner." I was on my own phone, checking messages. "It was a few hours later when we all met on the deck by the firepit and had a few drinks before going into the dining room for supper. After dinner and drinks, we decided to go fishing. Mullet fishing or scooping. We needed two boats, so we split up. Peter, Julian, and Rob took the gear.

Simon offered to help me get the other boat out of the shed.

"And Joseph and the ladies?"

"My dad stayed with them at the fire. He is still recovering from his bullet wound," Josh sipped his coffee and continued, "Simon and I got the boat out of the shed. We lifted it over our heads, boat upside down.

"What end of the boat were you at?"

"Bow… I led the way with Simon behind as our vision was obscured by the boat over our heads. I was familiar with the path. Gratefully, this protected us both from the blast. I never saw the explosion; we were stunned by the blast. It took me a while to figure out what happened. It was Lara and Mrs Perkins that pulled the boat off us."

"What were Lara and Simon's immediate reactions from what you saw?" Ed was pushing him for answers.

"Simon was in shock. He looked as confused as I did. Lara was frantically trying her best to help. I remember my father shouting out orders. It was pandemonium," Josh said, deflated.

"Josh, before this all happened, did you notice anyone leave the group for any reason."

"Grace and Mrs Perkins were in and out checking on catering staff. Simon left to make a call at one point. I took a call from Canada. There were a few bathroom breaks, nothing out of the ordinary."

"Thanks, Josh, that will be all for now. Please can you ensure no one leaves the lounge unsupervised," Ed verbally added the time the interview ended and stopped the recording.

Lara was relieved to see Josh enter the room. He looked directly at her just for a second, and that was all it took to reassure her he was fine.

"Okay, who's next," Ed said, looking around, "Ah, Ms Sheffield? Would you come with me?" Lara stood up, straightened her skirt, and briefly touched Josh's hand as she left the room with the Detective. Ed led the way. Lara was surprised by the cellar. She had not seen it before. As before, Ed went through the process with Lara. He gave his full name, time, and date. He introduced Lara Sheffield and had her verbally acknowledge her identity and that she agreed that the interview could be recorded. She did. "Lara, in your own words, state your recollection of events from the time you landed in George."

"We landed around mid-afternoon and came here; she said, looking around. Grace left snacks for us in the room, and we spent a few hours relaxing."

"Did you see anyone or talk to anyone?"

"No, but we stayed in the room until dinner time," she said, continuing, "I did give my sister a call to invite her and her husband, Rob, over for dinner."

"Where was Josh?"

"He was lying on the bed checking messages on his phone."

"We had a drink on the deck and then went in for dinner,"

"Tell me about that. Who was there?"

"Joseph, Josh, myself," she said, frowning a bit, recollecting, "Julian, Peter, Simon, Mrs Perkins, Grace and my sister and her husband Rob."

"Can you recall the movements of the guests during dinner?"

"Hmm, let me see. Grace was in and out. Josh took an overseas call. I went to the loo, oh yes, I bumped into Simon in the passage, going to the loo, I think. Stacey also used the lady's room. Other than that, we all had a lovely dinner."

"Until the explosion?" Ed added.

Lara sighed. "That was awful. One minute, we were laughing on the deck, and the next, I was trying to get the boat off Josh and Simon. I always imagined myself being in charge of myself and my reactions in a crisis. It was the opposite. I froze at the sight of the explosion, and panic set in. Not my finest hour. Joseph and Stacey took control and got us all moving." Lara wiped a tear off her cheek, "It is all a bit of a blur, I'm afraid."

"Thank you, Lara. You have been very helpful," Ed said verbally, adding the time the interview ended and stopping the recording. "That will be all for now."

Ed walked back to the lounge with Lara. It was Joseph's turn, and they both went down to the cellar. He pushed play on the recorder and gave his full name, time, and date. He introduced Joseph Dillion, who confirmed his identity and agreed that the interview could be recorded.

"Joseph, in your own words, state your recollection of events from the time you landed in George…"

Josh joined Lara at the bar with the rest of his guests. He made light of the circumstances and replenished their drinks. "It looks like we are in for a long night, I'm afraid. I do apologise for all this. Please feel free to make yourselves as comfortable as you need. We have games, books to read and chocolate cake to eat. The TV remote is also up for grabs." They all laughed.

CHAPTER 16

Joseph returned. One by one, they all got to see Chantilly's wine collection. By the time the last person left the room, Joseph was fast asleep in his chair. Simon was at the bar nursing yet another drink. Steve and the ladies were watching a movie. Rob and Josh were playing Backgammon. Wrinkles lay at Josh's feet. The fireplace lit the room up, creating a cosy ambience, but the mood was sombre.

Ed walked in looking weary. He put the basket of mobile phones on the coffee table. "Ladies and gentlemen, thank you for your cooperation," he said firmly as he proceeded to reach behind him and produced a set of handcuffs. A hush came over the room. You could hear a pin drop. Ed marched across the room, "Simon Fielding, you are under arrest for the murder of Julian Chambers and the attempted murder of Peter Patterson!"

Simon jumped to his feet. His face paled. He looked flabbergasted. Seemingly not surprised. His eyes said something entirely different as they darted towards all the possible exit routes. Josh and Rob were quick on their feet. Steve started to move from behind the bar. Ed continued holding his hand up as to say he had the situation under control, "There is nowhere to go, Mr Fielding."

"Oh really?" Simon hissed, pulling out a revolver and waving it pointedly around the room. There were gasps from the ladies. Joseph was now wide awake. With that, the room lit up like a nightclub as red and blue lights flashed through the glass sliding doors and windows.

"Put the gun down. It is over. We have the Estate surrounded," Ed said, pointing to the illuminated red dot on Simon's chest. Simon looked down; his shoulders dropped. Defeated, he put the gun on the bar counter and very slowly put his hands in the air. Ed moved swiftly to subdue and cuff Simon. The dejected man was handed over to the local Police.

Joseph was the first to react, "Detective, what the hell!? Was this Simon's doing?"

"Why would he want to kill one of us?" Josh said, astounded.

The room erupted, with the others voicing their surprise.

"Whoa, settle down, everyone... please," Ed said, motioning for them to quieten down, "all I can say is that thanks to Josh, we managed to search the rooms and check the mobile phones."

"The warrant helped," Josh added, laughing.

Ed continued, "We had our suspicions but needed the evidence, which we have now. There is no doubt that Simon planted the device. We believe his intention was to kill Josh. With Josh out of the equation, Mr Fielding no doubt believed that Joseph would put him in charge of JDE..."

"Not fucking likely!" Joseph blurted out.

"Dad!'

"What did this have to do with Blake?" Mrs Perkins said, looking confused.

"It looks like Mr Fielding was hired to finish the job that Blake had started. Suffice to say the evidence we have found is overwhelming."

"Can you at least tell us what evidence?" Josh said insistently.

Ed smiled. "As this is an ongoing investigation, there is a limit to what I can share at this point. As of this moment, we believe Simon was paid in Kruger Rands. We discovered a roll of twenty-five Kruger Rands in Simon's room. When we searched the cabin Blake was hiding out in, we found a wooden box clearly made to hold four rolls of Kruger Rands. One roll was missing. Simon is a greedy opportunist; my best guess is he was hoping to take advantage of a desperate situation and tried to work it in his favour – financially and professionally."

Ed looked around the room at a captured audience. Disbelief on their faces, each person present was silent as they absorbed what he had just told them.

Grace stood up and, with urgency, said, 'Detective, would you like a slice of chocolate cake?"

"I would love a slice of chocolate cake!" Ed said, smiling.

"What about the device. How do you know he planted the device?" Josh was looking for answers.

"The Forensics Report will reveal the evidence trail that links Simon to the device itself," Ed said, "for now, I'm not at liberty to reveal further details."

Josh nodded, considering what the Detective had just said. "What about a drink?" he offered, "I think we could all use one."

"Yes, why not? I am officially off duty," said Ed agreeably.

"Well, as much fun as this has been, we need to get home to the kids," Stacey said. Rob and Stacey said their goodbyes.

Chocolate cake and mostly coffee were had by the rest before a very exhausted household retired from what had been one heck of a bizarre evening.

The morning brought with it a sense of new beginnings. The hospital had called to say Peter was awake. He had a lengthy rehabilitation ahead, but his surgeon was confident he would make a full recovery. Steve had left early to check the weather and confirm flight plans before leaving for George Airport. Lara opted to stay with Josh and Wrinkles. Steve flew the rest of the team back to Joburg. Joseph informed Josh that Grace had decided to spend a week with him in Joburg to help with doctors' appointments and his recovery. *That was their story, and they were sticking to it,* Josh thought.

Lara decided to take advantage of the stand-alone Victorian bathtub. She lit all the candles she could find, added way too much bubble bath and let herself soak in the comforting warmth of the fragrant water. She lay there for ages, totally relaxed.

"Finally, we have the place to ourselves," Josh said, walking in with a glass of Champagne, "well, if you consider that all the people who want to kill me are dead or incarcerated."

"No, don't jinx it, Josh," Lara said playfully.

"Champagne?"

"Yummy, thanks."

"You look positively gorgeous," Josh said, kissing her gently on her lips.

"Are you going to join me?"

"Hmmm, tempting, but no. I have a surprise for you. When you're done, meet me in the cellar."

"Ahh, not the interrogation room?!" Lara wailed, frowning.

"Oh, ye of little faith, ma chérie!"

Lara finished her Champagne and reluctantly got out of the tub. *I could get used to this,* she thought, smiling. She went through Josh's wardrobe and found a white shirt to wear with her jeans. She pulled her hair loosely up in a messy bun, applied cream on her face, a little massacre, and some lip gloss. She looked into the mirror and was happy with her fresh, casual look. She sprayed a little perfume into the air and walked through it. *Subtle.* She made her way down the wooden staircase. The closer she got, the more she could hear music coming from the wine cellar. *She's Like the Wind* was playing, and Josh was singing at the top of his voice. He looked suitably embarrassed when he saw her standing at the door, arms folded, leaning against its frame. The wine cellar was now a far cry from the integration room it had been the previous evening. It had all the charm of a stone vineyard cellar, lit only by a string of small bulb lights and large, white church candles. The gentle music filled the chamber. The table was set up with a platter of grapes, strawberries, different cheeses and chocolate pralines. Josh greeted her with a hug and twirled her around the cellar.

"This is amazing, Josh, I love it. This place is awesome."

"It's one of my favourite places, I must say. And I did not want you to have an 'interrogation' memory of it," he said, holding his hand delicately on her chin.

Looking into her large, soft, blue eyes, he moved his thumb over her mouth and gently kissed it. "So, we are going to make new memories here. We are going to randomly select wine for tasting and food pairing." He placed a blindfold over her eyes, twirled her around, and stopped. "Okay, step to any side and point," he said, guiding her. Lara pointed to a classic Pinot Noir from the Stellenbosch wine route. Josh removed her blindfold and then uncorked the wine, explaining the fundamentals of wine tasting, "So ma chérie, generally we first look at the clarity of the wine. It should be clear if it's white, and if it is red, have a very deep colour," Josh poured the wine Lara selected into their glasses, picked his up, holding just the stem and continued, "Then we swirl the wine gently in the glass. Swirling releases the bouquet." Next, Josh instructed Lara, "Put your nose in the glass and smell the bouquet of the wine. This enhances the flavour and floral notes as it passes your lips onto your tongue. Sip the wine, slurp, and swallow." She did as she was told and took a sip, chuckling."

"You are laughing!" he said, smiling. "This is serious business."

"Serious? I do get it; can we taste this one?" Lara pointed.

"That is a dessert wine, which we will taste a little later."

They paired the delicious wine with Gruyere and strawberries dipped in chocolate. Next, Josh opened the Sauvignon Blanc, which paired with Goat's cheese. The night was surreal, with delectable pairings and perfect music choices. They danced to *Unchained Melody,* and Josh serenaded Lara with Lonestar's *Amazed.*

"I am pretty sure one should not drink the entire bottle when tasting the wine," Lara said, looking over at the empty bottle of Sauvignon Blanc.

"My cellar, my rules... but agreed, the rest can definitely wait for another time," Josh replied, laughing.

"Ooh, Brie, my favourite," Lara squealed, realising they'd missed a cheese, "we never tried that with anything."

"Ah-ha, now that calls for Champagne. I have a bottle of Moet just for this, and it pairs with Brie cheese beautifully."

"Okay, but just a wee bit, thanks," Lara said, squinting her nose up, showing the measure with her fingers.

Josh handed her half a glass of Champagne, "Ma chérie."

Lara giggled again, sipping her Champagne, "Do you speak French?"

"Oui mon amour, do you?" he asked, grinning.

"Sadly not, but it sounds so romantic. Say something else."

"Bois mon amour je suis sur le point de faire basculer ton monde."

"So, what did you say?" Lara whispered inquisitively. Josh leant over the table and kissed her gently, with subtle urgency.

"I could get accustomed to this," Lara whispered.

"Music to my ears," Josh replied with another kiss.

Lara took the last sip of her Champagne. Her eyes suddenly widened. She removed a round, brilliant diamond ring that was pinched between her lips. She looked at the ring and then at Josh. She watched as he got down on one knee. She caught her breath and smiled, tears rolling down her cheeks, "Oh, Josh."

He took her hand in his and sincerely said, "Je t'aime Lara Sheffield – will you marry me?"

** *The End* **

www.ingramcontent.com/pod-product-compliance
Lightning Source LLC
Chambersburg PA
CBHW071239250626
47163CB00001B/255